BOLAN'S WAY . . .

A chilling voice quietly commanded, "Stay there, Carlotti, and kiss your ass good-bye."

All Carlotti could see during that first dizzying instant was the big blaster and the black hand that held it. But it was not a Negro hand—it was artificially blackened. Then Carlotti saw glittering eyes. He was a big guy, black from head to toe—a goddam commando, no less, belts and guns and grenades and all kinds of shit strung all over him. And, no, it wasn't a Mardi Gras costume.

All hope departed, like the final flaring of a shooting star, and the Boss of Sin felt his knees buckling, his whole frame sagging. The guy jerked him back upright and pressed something into his hand—the clincher, the medal of death.

It was not hope that spoke but desperation as Carlotti pleaded, "God, don't do this, Bolan. Don't do it!"

D1010370

THE EXECUTIONER SERIES

THE EXECUTIONER

New Orleans Knockout

by
Don Pendleton

PINNACLE BOOKS • NEW YORK CITY

THE EXECUTIONER: NEW ORLEANS KNOCKOUT

Copyright © 1974 by Pinnacle Books, Inc.

An original Pinnacle Books edition, published for the first time anywhere.

ISBN: 0-523-00475-3

First printing, November 1974
Second printing, March 1975

Printed in the United States of America

PINNACLE BOOKS, INC.
275 Madison Avenue
New York, N.Y. 10016

For Jack Petro—
whose name is not really that,
and whose town is not really New Orleans—
a hell of a guy who knows all about wallbanging
and large living.

dp

Right is founded not in opinion
but in nature.
—Cicero

For Man's grim Justice goes its way,
　And will not swerve aside:
It slays the weak, it slays the strong,
　It has a deadly stride.
—Oscar Wilde, *Ballard of Reading Gaol*

The Mob can't be allowed a free ride. They have
to pay the tab, like everyone else. If I'm the only
collector, then so be it. But I collect in blood.
Mafia blood. And the line forms everywhere.
—Mack Bolan, THE EXECUTIONER

PROLOGUE

"Why defend a front line 8,000 miles away when the real enemy is chewing up everything you love at home?" This was Mack Bolan's understanding of the problem—the organized crime problem in America.

He had been a career soldier with twelve years of service and several Asian combat tours behind him. He was a skilled armorer and an expert marksman with every personal weapon in his country's arsenal. He was also a "kill" specialist—a highly trained and remarkably proficient penetrator of enemy zones. Coupled with all this was the basic man himself— the nerveless, self-commanding, highly intelligent war machine who had earned his code name "the Executioner" by making ninety-eight confirmed kills among the enemy hierarchy in Southeast Asia. In the words of a former commanding officer, Mack Bolan was "a very deadly dude and a terrible weapon in our psychological counterwar."

Then Sergeant Bolan had been called home to bury his own dead—mother, father, kid sister—victims of another sort of human savagery. And the awesome focus of this "terrible weapon" shifted to the "home front." A new war was born—in the most savage jungle of all.

The Executioner was taking on the Mafia!

1 : REMEMBRANCE

It was a perfect spot for an ambush. The road was narrow, winding through dense woods, remote —seldom traveled at this hour of night. The terrain was flat, swampy; this was bayou country. Climbing vines clung to the trees and trailed from their branches, interlocking in the air to form an unending network that seemed to encompass the entire forest—bringing it all together in a living unity.

Yeah. Jungle country, American style. Impenetrable except by water and the thin thread of macadam highway.

It was Mack Bolan's kind of place.

He was rigged for heavy combat. A black suit as snug as his own skin covered him from neck to ankles. Hands and face were blackened. Supple swamp-moccasins reached to just below the knees. Military web circled his waist to support the head weapon, a .44 AutoMag, as well as other deadly items of ordnance. Other belts crossed the chest like bandoliers but were narrower and bore another selection of munitions. A black Beretta Brigadier rode shoulder harness beneath the left arm, and an Israeli weapon—an *Uzi* submachine gun—dangled from a neck strap.

On the ground beside him were four harmless-looking fiberglass tubes. They were officially designated "light antitank weapon"—or LAW—and they were far from harmless. The Disposable Age's answer to the bazooka, these prepackaged armor-piercing rockets came in their own throwaway launchers and could handle most any battlefield job.

The dawn was still an hour away. All the preparations for battle had been completed, and there was nothing to do now but wait. As was his style, Mack Bolan's preparations had been elaborate and exhaustive. A pro did not leave the smallest detail to chance. Mack Bolan was certainly a pro. He had lived in this swamp for more than a week. He knew the roadways and waterways, and he had mocked-up this operation for dry runs over and over again. He knew what had to be done and how—and he knew full well the elements of chance and the percentages for success or failure—which, in Bolan's line of work, meant living or dying.

But, yes, it was Mack Bolan's kind of place. He remembered his surprise, some years back, at finding a jungle within a march of Saigon. And the Cajun kid—what was his name?—the one that stepped into the VC snare trap and died with a stake through his belly—Clautier, yeah, nice kid—Clautier had remarked that it was no big deal. There were jungles within walking distance of New Orleans, denser than anything he'd seen yet in Vietnam.

4

Bolan hadn't really believed the kid then. Now he believed.

An armadillo waddled onto the highway and paused for an unemotional inspection of the black-clad human interloper before continuing on to the other side.

Smart kid, sure, move on. You're in a war zone. All the armor in Louisiana won't keep you safe here —so move it on out. Bolan grinned. Some kind of funny-looking animal—like a possum with armor plating. Not funny, though . . . *tragic*. The world of nature had abandoned the armor-plating experiment long before man came on the scene. Still the armadillo lingered on. Bolan's gaze fell on the armor-piercing rockets in their neat little fiberglass tubes. Sure . . . and the idea lingered on in the minds of men.

The smile faded from the warrior's face as he took final stock of the situation. Any minute now a convoy would be rounding that curve up there at Point Able and lining into this brief straightaway. He'd clocked them on three previous runs and there'd been no deviation from the routine. It would take them ten seconds to reach Bolan's position at Point Baker. In another ten seconds, if they were incredibly lucky, they'd be scooting around the next curve at Point Charlie. In the lead would be a Cadillac limousine—one of the big jobs with jumpseats and a full crew of eight gunners. Certain barely noticeable alterations to the body lines revealed that it was armor-plated like the armadillo, but much more so.

Close behind the point vehicle would be the Brinks-type truck carrying the goodies—three days' receipts from the string of mob-owned joints along

5

the Mississippi Gulf Coast—black money from the casinos and the take from girlie operations, contraband booze, the drug scene, illicit rackets of every kind. This particular shipment would also include fifty kilos of uncut heroin plucked from a Central American banana boat at Gulfport just three hours earlier and destined now for a powder plant in the French Quarter at New Orleans. Manned gunports in the van indicated a minimum of three heavily armed guards inside.

Bringing up the rear would be a second limousine identical in all respects to the lead vehicle.

About nineteen guns, at least—including automatic weapons. And some of the meanest boys south of the Mason-Dixon, old man Vannaducci's best.

Through a nice piece of official larceny, each of them toted "special police" credentials. The armored truck was legitimately registered, licensed, bonded, etc. And still they made their runs along the back trails like the scurrying vermin they really were.

Vermin, sure. These boys were Mafia, each of them sworn in blood. And each of them was going to die in that sworn blood. As for their black money—it was going to get liberated . . . into the Executioner's war chest, about $300,000 by conservative estimate. And people were still saying that crime doesn't pay. It paid, all right—for the organized psychopaths swaggering about their vicious little kingdoms of syndicated cannibalism—it paid to the annual national tune of about $70 *billion*—more than the top three U.S. corporations combined—a GNP higher than most nations of the world.

The Dixie mob was getting its fair share of that.

6

The boys had been having things their way in this area for much too long. The Executioner's gaze had been focused on Vannaducci's little empire for some time—and he'd decided it was time for the universe to present the bill to Uncle Van and all his little savages.

The Mafia presence here went back a long way—further back than most people might think. As early as 1890 they'd murdered a chief of police who couldn't be bought, then bought a jury to get the killers off scot-free. An irate citizenry then lynched the bunch. Hysterical repercussions from that, around the country as well as abroad, saw an embarrassed U.S. Government officially apologizing and even paying damages to the Italian government to still the furor. Naturally, the Dixie mob promptly returned to business as usual, raping and looting the economy of the South with renewed zeal—and nobody had really presented them with a bill of complaint since.

So now the note had matured. The collector had come. It was time to pay the tab for nearly a century of plunder. "The city that care forgot" had not been forgotten by everyone.

The Executioner cared.

His fingers traced the outline of the little transistorized pocket detonator that would officially announce the Battle for New Orleans. He was ready. The jungle was ready. And the glow of approaching headlamps was now sweeping into the curve at Point Able.

The time had come to throw the first punch for the New Orleans knockout.

7

The wheelman reflexively jabbed an elbow toward Jimmy Lista and growled, "Boss!"

Lista, the convoy boss, jerked upright in the seat, and his eyes flared as he muttered, "Yeah. What? Why the slowdown?"

"Something's ahead. On the road."

"Accident or what?"

"Could be," the wheelman replied. "Looks like railroad flares, just around the curve."

Lista snatched up the mike and spat hasty instructions into the radio net. "Peckers up!" He was wide awake now but still fighting the cobwebs from his eyes. "Close up, close it up! I want a tight one-two-three."

While the taut responses crackled in from the vehicles that followed, the wheelman remarked, "I don't see nothing but the flares, boss. It looks funny. I don't like it."

"Me neither," Lista agreed. "Boot this thing in the ass." He snarled into the radio mike: "We're running! Stay up our ass!" To the men in the seats behind him he commanded, "Weapons up and ready! Look alive now!"

The next few seconds were kaleidoscopic. Though everything seemed to happen at once, a frozen frame replay would bring the events to focus in the following sequence:

With a strong but smooth acceleration the armor-plated limousine surged forward into the straightaway.

A gunner in the rear seat excitedly wondered, "What if it's cops? Whatta we do if—"

Lista yelled back, "You crazy? With a hot box of horse back there? We're stopping for nobody!"

8

A bright flash lit up the side of the road just ahead as a huge tree came crashing to the ground across the roadway.

The wheelman yelped, "Christ!" and stood on his brakes.

Lista screamed, "You dumb . . . !" and began fighting the driver for control of the vehicle, evidently intending to veer around the blockade.

The wheelman was protesting, "No, boss! There's nothing out there but swamp!"

The men in the rear seats were being flung about by the wild swerving of the vehicle. They were swearing and exclaiming—and one man's weapon discharged accidentally, the reverberations from that blast adding to the panic and confusion of the moment.

Then they were sliding into the felled tree, hitting it broadside, rebounding—and the heavy truck that had been faithfully "right up their ass" was crunching in from the other side.

In perhaps his final flaring instant of electric awareness, Lista caught a glimpse of a tall figure in black loping along the eerily lighted roadway with a weird object slung over one shoulder—and in that instant Jimmy Lista knew.

"Oh, Christ!" he groaned. "It's that guy!"

And then hell really fell in.

The big cypress had been carefully selected, restraining vines hacked away, then the tree trunk drilled and charged with enough plastics to ensure a clean and instant drop. Detonation was perfect, and the fall just as Bolan wanted it. There would not

9

have been time, even had Bolan been so inclined, to yell, "Timber!"

They came into it on a cadenced count, practically bumper to bumper, the lead vehicle trying to change the game at the final moment only to slide in sideways on screaming rubber. The other two vehicles promptly plowed into the wreckage—and the battle was half-won right there.

Bolan's set position had been about fifty yards in advance of the roadblock point—that is, downrange; he was now behind the procession. A second or two before the moment of impact, the blitz artist was up and running, closing on the scene with studied timing and with massive firepower at his ready disposal. A tree across the road could momentarily stop that bunch, but it could not neutralize them—not without the most incredible luck, and Bolan was not a warrior to stake the success of an operation on mere luck.

But even the most meticulous planner could not foresee every eventuality—and the very worst had come from that pile-up of vehicles, from Bolan's point of view. The heavy truck had punched into the side of the lead Caddy, screwing it around so that a surviving headlamp was throwing a beam of light along the back track, directly along Bolan's only possible path of advance. The problem was, of course, twofold. The beam was both blinding and illuminating him—and the resolution of the problem cost a couple of numbers to his timing. He was still some thirty yards downrange when he halted and drew the AutoMag, coolly sighted along the ventilated barrel, and squeezed off a 240-grain resolution. The big bullet thundered along that beam of light and wiped it out. But already there were sounds of re-covery down there—cautious cries in the night, the whirring of a starter coaxing a dead engine, vehicle doors springing open.

A couple of numbers off the count, yeah. He'd hoped to catch them stunned and stupid. But now . . .

Not much threat from the lead vehicle. It was a mess. People in there were yelling for help, and one guy in particular was screaming bloody murder.

The armored van seemed none the worse for the pile-up, except that the engine would not respond. Gunports were manned and obviously ready with ugly snouts protruding and waiting for a target.

It was the rear limousine that posed the gravest danger. The engine hood had popped open, and there was broken glass strewn about, but that seemed to be the extent of the damage. A couple of guys were staggering from the open doors of that one, and they both had Thompsons.

Bolan moved warily into position and dropped to one knee, jettisoning all but one LAW. The boys with the choppers found him just one breathless sec-ond after he'd aligned the pop-up sights and sent a whoosher streaking into the rear section of their ve-hicle. It penetrated with a doomsday clap that blew a halo of hellfire to envelop all three vehicles and to make instant tumbling torches of the two machine-gunners.

So now they were stunned and stupid again—those who were still alive. Someone over there in hell was screaming for heavenly mercy. Bolan sent some, in the form of another whizzing rocket that smacked into the crumpled passenger compartment of the

11

lead vehicle. All four wheels of the Caddy left the ground with that one, and the gas tank joined the act just as the vehicle touched down again. The secondary gasoline explosion welded the limousine to the nose of the van, sent displaced chunks of auto-motive steel hurtling through the night, and spread a rushing pool of flames beneath the armored truck. A gunport there was hastily abandoned; an instant later a ventilation hatch creaked open, and Bolan could hear the sounds of panic inside.

He was in motion again, reading the situation in a wary approach to the blast zone. Both Cadillacs were demolished. Twisted and mutilated bodies, some of them flaming, littered the whole area. Gaso-line-fed flames were enveloping the armored van and all four wheels were ablaze.

And now there were no human sounds to disturb the night.

The armored truck was fast becoming a bake oven, no doubt of that. The men inside could probably sweat it out for another minute or so—but Bolan knew that there could be no fight left in them now.

It was done.

He abandoned the remaining LAWs and closed on the situation with *Uzi* at the ready. At his approach, the driver of the van screamed out through licking flames: *"Okay! I'm coming out! Don't shoot!"*

The ice-water tones of the Executioner flowed across the hellground. "So come. Hit the ground run-ning and don't look back."

The guy tumbled to the ground and lay there for a moment beating out flames on his clothing, then staggered to his feet and floundered into the marshy

12

land at the side of the road to disappear into the night.

The boys in the vault must have been watching. The back door immediately swung open and a panicky voice called out, *"Us, too! We surrender!"*

"Same deal," was the cold response from the edge of hell.

Three uniformed men leapt out of there as if in a single movement, arms raised, coughing, and soaked with perspiration.

"Not the swamp," Bolan instructed. "Down the road. Fast as you can move it."

He watched them till they were out of sight, then quickly entered the vault, grabbed the goodies, left his calling card, and withdrew.

After all was said and done, then, right on the numbers.

And, yes, Bolan remembered . . . many things. So would the New Orleans mob. They would remember all of the Executioner campaigns along that twisted and bloody trail that began at Pittsfield and broadened at places like Los Angeles, Chicago, New York, Miami, San Francisco, Detroit, and at many stops and pauses beyond and between—and, sure, they would know. They would understand that this quick punch to the gut in a Louisiana swamp was but the prelude to a blitzkrieg war that would soon engulf this entire region.

They would remember, they would know, and they would be falling all over their asses to get set for it.

The Executioner had come to the town that care forgot.

2: ANGLE OF APPROACH

A growing number of emergency vehicles were grouped on either side of the disaster zone, and the entire area was brightly illuminated by police floodlights when the rackets specialist from NOPD, Jack Petro, arrived on the scene.

He left his vehicle at the western fringe, sandwiched between an ambulance and a rescue unit, and scrambled to the top of the barricade to view the incredible scene on the other side. A uniformed state cop recognized the new arrival and walked carefully along the trunk of the fallen swamp cypress to join him.

"Ever see anything like this before, Lieutenant?" the trooper inquired with a wry smile.

The detective pushed his hat back and surveyed the scene with hands on hips. "Tell me what it is," he replied quietly, "and I'll tell you if I have."

"It seems that old man Vannaducci got his tables turned," the trooper said, seeming to enjoy the idea.

"Then, no. I've never seen anything like it."

Petro stepped down to the combat zone and moved carefully among the wreckage, pieces of which were still smoldering. Medics were moving busily about in three-man teams, while a man Petro recognized as the St. Tammany coroner officiated over a mounting collection of human remains—some on shrouded litters, others in plastic bags.

He found the chief deputy sheriff inside the armored truck. "Thanks for the call," the New Orleans cop said by way of greeting.

The deputy did not look up from his task. "Thought you'd be interested," he grunted, and went on taking Polaroid pictures of the interior. "This truck belongs to Vannaducci. Another five minutes and they'd have been inside your jurisdiction."

"Yeah," Petro agreed sourly. "What's it look like? Who did it?"

"Looks like a company of marines did it," the deputy replied, turning to his visitor with a strained smile. "The tree was dropped with an explosive charge. My expert says it's a very professional job. Remote-detonated, probably electronically. These vehicles were in motion and moving fast when the thing crashed down right across their path. No chance to stop or avoid. They hit at high speed and crunched together—following too close.

"Let's get out of here." The deputy moved past Petro and stepped to the ground.

The detective took a quick look around, then followed suit.

"Still hot in there," the cop observed, tugging at his shirt collar. "You can imagine what it was like immediately after the hit. All three vehicles are armor-plated. The two sedans were under attack by bazookas—or something on that order. Opened 'em up like tin cans. The gas tanks ruptured and built a hot fire under *this* tin can. Wonder it didn't blow sky high."

A uniformed cop wearing asbestos gloves and a padded helmet was moving purposefully toward the chief deputy. Petro checked what he was about to say, yielding to the new arrival. The guy was carrying a couple of interesting-looking tubes.

"Here's your answer, Chief," he reported solemnly. "Found 'em laying in the reeds just off the road—about thirty yards downrange. I marked the spot."

"What the hell are they?" the deputy asked, his nose wrinkling.

"Rocket launchers. Army calls them LAWs. Self-contained units, armor-piercing, high-explosive projectiles. One of 'em will stop a light tank."

"Take 'em over to the lab truck."

"Right."

"There you go," the chief deputy told his visitor from New Orleans.

"Where the hell do these people get military ordnance?" Petro wondered aloud.

"Just about anywhere. If you know the angles. I'd say that our man knows all of them."

"*Our* man?"

"Uh huh. Left his trademark all over the job. Didn't even try to conceal it. Even left witnesses."

"You mean somebody survived this?" Petro asked quietly.

"You bet. The driver and three guards from the truck are okay. The guy let 'em go."

16

"Okay. I'll bite. *What* guy, dammit?"

"I'll get to that. Let me fill you in some first. We got this anonymous report a few minutes past three —man's voice, cold, hard, methodical, gave directions to the tenth of a mile. We dispatched a car to investigate. Place was still ablaze when our officers arrived. Four survivors hiding in the bayou, submerged from the neck down—one of them with second-degree burns covering twenty percent of his body. Shows you how shook they were. Hit the water and stayed there until our unit arrived. They—"

"I'll want to talk to them," Petro said.

"Sure. But maybe I have you a better one than that. If he makes it."

"Another survivor?"

"Maybe. We evacuated him by helicopter. Guess who?"

Petro's eyes jerked impatiently. "Who?"

"Your crown prince of Bourbon Street—Jimmy Lista. It seems that he was bossing this run. So you know what that means."

Sure, Petro knew what that meant. A mob money run. "How big a haul?"

"Nobody's saying. But you know how the estimates run. Maybe as much as half a mil."

Petro whistled and nervously lit a cigarette. "Okay," he said, breaking a heavy silence. "So they hit the old man for maybe half a mil, and there'll be heads rolling in New Orleans when he finds out. So who did it? Who are they?"

The chief deputy was gazing across the disaster zone, a tense smile arranging his features into a sort

17

of half-worried, half-humorous expression. "Would you believe . . . a *him?*"

"*One* guy?" Petro's hands went back to his hips, and he swiveled his torso in another evaluation of the hit zone. His face suddenly underwent a radical alteration. "Oh, hell," he commented quietly, resignedly.

"Yeah. That's the guy. Left his calling card in the truck." The chief deputy produced a small envelope, withdrew a folded Kleenex, and carefully unwrapped the "calling card"—a military marksman's medal.

"Well . . ." Petro exhaled noisily. "I guess it was inevitable. The guy had to get around to us sooner or later. You put out the alert yet?"

"Not yet. Call it an official courtesy—I wanted you to see it first. The guy is, uh, probably into your jurisdiction by now. You got a complete file?"

Petro nodded. "In spades."

"I'm glad it's you instead of me," the sheriff said, smiling grimly. "We're just not equipped over here for a Mack Bolan war."

"Who is?" Petro observed quietly.

Moments later he was speeding back to town and sending the word ahead via radio.

The Executioner, for God's sake, was undoubtedly marching on New Orleans. Along with several hundred thousand other transients. What a time for a Mack Bolan visit! Tomorrow was Fat Tuesday, a day of local insanity better known by its French name, *Mardi Gras*. Unless Jack Petro missed his guess, it was going to be the fattest damn Tuesday in the city's history.

3: ANGLE OF THRUST

It was an uncharacteristically early awakening for Thomas Carlotti, the acknowledged "boss of sin" in greater New Orleans. There'd been a time, of course —and not too many years earlier, at that—when most of Carlotti's waking moments had been spent with the night. A guy who had to hustle those streets for a buck had to run when and where the action was. Carlotti no longer hustled the streets. Now he hustled the hustlers, pushed the buttons and pulled the strings, orchestrating a network of prostitution and gambling houses that encompassed all of New Orleans and her suburbs.

Carlotti was thirty-five, medium height, well built and muscular. He was a flashy dresser. Even his shirts and underwear were hand-tailored—and it was said that the Mafia chieftain cared more for his wardrobe than for any other thing in life. His shoes were specially ordered from "my little old bootmaker" in Rome. A barber visited the Royal Street manse three times a week to maintain the well-coiffed locks. It was gossiped quietly that Carlotti was impressed by his superficial resemblance to singer Enzo Stuarti and tried diligently to strengthen that resemblance.

Carlotti didn't like to be awakened in the gray hours of the morning. He'd seen enough sunrises from street level to last a lifetime. He preferred to arise about ten, several hours behind the rest of the household, when things were humming along and filled with life and movement.

God, but he hated to wake up to a still house.

"What the hell is this?" he growled to his night man, Scooter Favia. "What d'ya mean coming in here at a time like this? Turn off that goddam light. Use the lamp—over there—that lamp over there."

The houseman moved silently to obey the instructions. Scooter had been with Carlotti throughout his rise to power, was reputed to be a nerveless trigger-man and a remorseless killer whenever such actions were likely to please his boss. He had served others, many others, during his thirty years behind the gun —with about the same measure of faithful service.

Carlotti's "broad for the night"—an unnaturally high-bosomed stripper from one of the Bourbon Street tourist traps—stirred sleepily, then sat bolt up-right. Carlotti scowled at her and shoved her back down.

"Get those silicone boobs under cover," he scolded. "What, you want to get poor old Scooter all tore up and nothing to work with?"

The girl, a blonde of about twenty, giggled and flipped the sheet up to cover her head.

The boss of New Orleans vice life pushed his own nude body from the bed and unhurriedly reached

20

for a karate-style wraparound. He slipped into it and belted it loosely, lit a cigarette, told the girl to "Stay right there, tiger," and went over to join his bodyguard at the door.

"Now what?" he asked Favia.

"Zeno called," the houseman reported in a hushed voice. "Mr. Vannaducci wants you out at the farm. Soon as you can get there."

"At this hour? It's—what . . . ?"

"Little past four. That's what Zeno said, Tommy. Soon as you can get there. He sounded worried."

"That rotten shit of a prosecutor again!" Carlotti fumed.

"I don't think so. This sounded different. Zeno's calling all the bosses. It's a summit."

"Aw, aw, aw," Carlotti commented, shaking his head with disgust. "What the hell is it this time, I wonder!"

He dropped the cigarette into an ashtray and moved hastily toward his dressing room, pausing in mid-stride to turn a troubled gaze toward the bed—as though remembering some unfinished business there. He snapped his fingers at Favia and instructed, "Get that outta here. Give her some breakfast money."

Favia went dutifully to the bed, hauled the girl out, scooped up her clothing from a chair, and carried the works out, tucked loosely beneath a massive arm—the girl wide-eyed but silent.

Carlotti called from the dressing room doorway, "Be a good kid and I'll phone you some time."

He shrugged out of the karate wrap and threw it at a wooden peg on the wall as he strode past. It held for a moment then slid free and dropped to

21

the carpeted floor as its owner moved on toward the darkened bathroom. He halted, returned, bent down to retrieve the robe—then froze, bent over like that, something hard and ominous pressing against the crown of his head.

A chilling voice quietly commanded, "Stay there, Carlotti, and kiss your ass goodbye."

At such a moment, something strange happens within the human psyche—even to a bruised and calloused one such as that of Thomas Carlotti, the Boss of Sin. A cacophony of conflicting emotions bristled into that moment of doom—anger, betrayal, hate, even repentance—but the greatest of all was sadness, an overriding and consuming sadness that contemplated the fall of domain, the final failure, life and all its grand plans for the future ending here and now.

It was all there in that ragged voice, as he asked the question that had already been answered. "What the hell is this? Whattaya want?"

"Just you, Carlotti," was the icy response.

Hope dies hard, especially in the doomed breast. Still contemplating his own knobby knees, Carlotti gasped, "If it's a contract, I'll buy it out. Double your money. Triple it. Hell, *you* say."

"This contract was written in the stars, guy." Strong fingers curled into the hair of his head, straightened him, spun him, slammed him face-to against the wall—all the while the steady pressure at the crown of the head reminding him to be still, stay cool, keep hoping.

"If this is a gag, hey, you're just in time for Mardi Gras."

"No gag, Carlotti."

"This is crazy, guy. I got a dozen boys under this roof."

"Five."

"Huh?"

"You had five, Carlotti."

"And they're light sleepers—uh—*had?*"

"Uh huh. They're heavy sleepers now. All but Favia. He'll keep."

The underboss was coming totally unstuck. This wasn't fair—for God's sake, it just wasn't fair. All those years on the street—all that work and sweat and tears—and just now when everything was coming together so beautifully . . . "Not fair!" he groaned.

"I'm not your judge, guy."

"Who *is* then?"

"*You* are. I'm just the judgment."

Carlotti laughed, at the edge of hysteria. "I don't get that. Who sent you?"

"You sent me. And I don't expect you to understand it." The pistol muzzle slid slowly along the back of Carlotti's head, boring up just above the vertebrae. "Ten seconds to tell it all goodbye, Tommy."

"*Wait, dammit, wait!* We can work this out!"

"I don't think so." The guy spun him around, the pistol tracking on with the movement to punch in just beneath the chin.

All Carlotti could see during that first dizzying instant was the big blaster, black, tipped with an ominous bulb at the muzzle end—a silencer—and the black hand that held it. But it was not a Negro hand—it was artificially blackened, and extending away from it was more blackness, then glittering eyes—a big guy, black from head to toe—a fuckin' commando, no less, belts and guns and grenades and all kinds of shit strung all over him. And, no, it wasn't Mardi Gras.

All hope departed, like the final flaring of a shooting star, and the Boss of Sin felt his knees buckling, his whole frame sagging. The guy jerked him back upright and pressed something into his hand—sure, the clincher, the medal of death.

It was not hope that spoke but desperation, as Carlotti pleaded, "God, don't do this, Bolan. Don't do it."

"Give me an alternative," the iceman replied.

"What?"

"What do you love more than life, Carlotti?"

"Nothing!" He was scrabbling now, hanging on like a drowning man to a lifeline. "Listen, I revere life. I *revere* it. I never burned a guy in my life, not ever! I don't deserve *this*, Bolan—I really don't."

"What do you deserve then?"

"God, I—a guy don't get the chair for *purse* snatching, Christ's sake."

The big guy was just standing there, watching him with those goddam eyes—didn't even seem to be breathing—no expression on the face, like carved in ice, head cocked a bit to one side.

Then Carlotti knew: the guy's mind hadn't been on *him* at all. The legends were true, the stories were straight—the guy was some kind of superhuman. He'd heard or *felt* big Favia moving through the house downstairs and starting up the stairway. The creaking step near the top was Carlotti's first awareness of the approach—but this impassive bastard had already sprung another gun from his hip, a big silver autoloader with a ventilated barrel, easily a foot long, that went smoothly and quickly inside Carlotti's mouth, pinning his head to the wall from the inside.

Scooter hit the bedroom door on the run and with a lot of noise, but all Carlotti could see at the moment was the silent black blaster extended at arm's length, angling into that confrontation.

Favia had started yelling from the other side of the door: "Boss! Sam and all his boys got sliced in their beds, throats cut! We better . . ."

By this time, Scooter Favia was through the doorway and hastily applying brakes, eyes bugging at that scene just inside the dressing room, his snub-nosed .38 waving in the air and instinctively falling into a firing lineup.

The black blaster gave out a little *pa-tooey* and bucked slightly in the tall guy's big fist. Carlotti swore he saw that bullet hurtle out of there and thwack into big Favia's forehead squarely between the eyes.

The old comrade and faithful gun toter went down without a sound, pitching over backwards through the doorway and out of sight.

Carlotti's knees again gave way. He broke a tooth on the silver pistol before he could recover himself —then like magic it was gone and back in the guy's holster at the hip—the silent blaster, a bit warm now, back in position at Carlotti's throat—and that cold voice, as calm as ever, was saying, "Okay, I'll take a note, Carlotti. A mortgage on this revered life of yours. I'll take it written on the torn shreds of your oath of *Omerta*. You've got about two heart-beats to decide."

What decide? Carlotti thought. "You want me to

stool for you?" he whispered, at the ragged edge of human endurance.

"That, or die for me. One heartbeat left, beautiful."

Hell, sure, *what* decide! Die now for sure or die later, probably when the organization discovers that Thomas Carlotti, heir apparent to the invisible golden throne of New Orleans, had shitted out on the sacred oath of silence.

Perspiration appeared suddenly in a film across his forehead and dripped from his upper lip. Moisture returned to the mouth and unstuck the throat. He felt like laughing and crying all at once. So this was how it felt to get a reprieve just as you were being buckled into the chair. The naked mafioso looked into those glittering eyes and squeezed the little iron cross until it cut into the flesh of his palm, then his gaze dropped, he took a shuddering breath and told the big cold bastard, "I'm not ready to kiss it goodbye, Bolan. You've got yourself a note."

What Bolan had, at that moment, was his angle of penetration for the assault on New Orleans. It was, indeed, precisely what he had come for.

4: ANNOUNCEMENT

It was a grim and restrained group of Mafia chiefs who were gathering at the former sugar plantation on the old River Road in southwest New Orleans. The site was now the home and showplace estate of Marco Vannaducci, acknowledged "greatgodfather" of Southern crime syndication—lately a man trying almost desperately to display a face of respectability to his community. "Emergency" sessions called at weird hours, such as this one, had become almost a standard routine in recent months—a circumstance that had begun to wear the nerves and patience of the New Orleans hierarchy of organized crime.

Vannaducci had been "in trouble" for some time, and just about everybody knew it. He was old and sickly. He had never been known as an iron-fisted administrator; his territories had been getting out of hand for years, with ambitious young Turks jostling to the forefront and competing with one another for the ripe pickings abounding everywhere in the empire that stretched from Florida to Texas, from the Gulf to St. Louis, and in virtually every facet of enterprise—legal and illegal—known to the American economy. There was the shipping of the second largest port in the country, the unions, the oil, natural gas, pipelines, warehousing and trucking, banking, construction, horseracing, organized sports—and, of course, backing it all was old New Orleans herself, an aging harlot-queen who smiled beneficently on every vice known to man.

Other Mafia families had often cast lecherous glances at the Vannaducci empire, but none had ventured, yet, to encroach upon it. Vannaducci himself was the man and the power here, and all knew it. His "ins" were legion, his influence everywhere. The wealth of the area had been pyramiding steadily for years; the entire South was booming—Little Rock, Atlanta, Memphis, Nashville, Jackson, Montgomery—all were exploding at the seams and running over with the boom of an unprecedented expansionist economy—and Marco Vannaducci was present in some guise in all of it.

On two past occasions when the *amici* in the North had seemed ready to risk interfamily confrontation with an expedition into the golden honeypot of the South, Vannaducci had anticipated their intentions and headed them off with conciliatory "grants" of silent partnership in various new enterprises, an arrangement in which outside *capi* were allowed to invest moderate sums and reap windfall rewards—sometimes on an overnight basis and without even knowing the identity of the enterprise. Vannaducci himself consciously realized that such

28

arrangements were outright payments of tribute to his brothers in the North; so, too, did they. Some of them had begun referring to the old man jokingly as "the broker"—and, of course, such disrespect had a way of getting back to its object.

So, sure, Vannaducci knew. But he had learned long ago that false pride could be a hell of an expensive way to kid oneself. He was old and sick. The feds were after his hide, wanted to deport him. His own young Turks were staking out their inheritances and busting their britches to step in and take over. A man in this position could tolerate a bit of disrespect from outside territories if it would help keep the peace a little longer.

"A little longer" was all Marco Vannaducci had to hope for, anyway. Either by old age, by assassination, or by deportation—his end was in view.

Of all the alternatives, the one feared most by Marco was deportation. This was home, this town. He'd lived here most of his long life. He'd grown rich here, gained "respect" here—it was the place he chose to die. A man of seventy-five thought of such things: a place to die, a place to be buried and remembered. Marco Vannaducci would be buried in his own tomb, on his own land, in his own country —not, by God, in some crumbling little cemetery in Central America—and by no means in a foreign and faraway land like Italy, born there or not.

And now they were saying that this Bolan boy had come roaring into town. Well . . . Marco was not afraid of Mack Bolan—not *mortally* afraid. He had respect for the boy, sure. You just naturally had to respect a boy with a reputation like his. But an old man who'd lived through seventy-five years on sheer grit and cunning knew that things were not always as they appeared—reputations were not always entirely earned. Sometimes they grew by their own weight. But that wasn't the point. The point was that the empire needed no rattling and shaking —not by anybody—especially not by a boy who operated the way this Bolan was said to operate. Reputation or not, the guy always left a wake behind him like a battleship, and in that wake were always a lot of ruined enterprises, bleeding territories, dead men, confusion, chaos. This was the last thing in the world desired by a man of seventy-five who was just trying to hold it all together long enough to die decently in it.

And Marco was hoping that the newest "Bolan flap" would turn out to be a false alarm.

Those men now gathering downstairs were the most trusted lieutenants of his empire. Some were pretty young, sure—and maybe one or two were still a bit wet behind the ears—but they all believed in Marco, looked up to him, trusted him, and you just couldn't say that about all the boys he had under his wing. Some were just so much rotten shit. Marco knew that, had always known it, even when he made them, he'd known it. But every empire needed a certain amount of rotten shit in it. It kept the others on their toes, gave vigor to the whole organization.

But these men gathering downstairs . . . well, now, Marco Vannaducci would bet the whole empire on them—hell, he was doing just that! They were men. *Men!* Not skulking hyenas, not belly-sliding snakes in the grass, not buzzards circling to strip the bones of a sick old man who wanted only to die with honor and dignity on his own plot of turf. *Men!*

These men would hold the empire together.

And they would, by God, *inherit* it. *All* of it!

Such were the thoughts of the tired old man as he went to the curtained French doors to gaze upon the grounds that had come to mean so much to him. Magnolia trees, beautiful, standing in state and lining that long and picturesque drive from the old River Road—oleanders, pure poison from root to bud, but beautiful in their season—mimosa, tulip, weeping willow—acres of lawn and bush and flower gardens. Some day it would all be a public park— Vannaducci Park—yeah, a fitting place for a man of dignity to be buried.

Dawn shadows were just beginning to creep across those grounds, and something was moving with them—a car, swinging hesitantly off the old River Road and moving slowly along the lane. Vannaducci watched with vague apprehension as the vehicle halted at the gate, passed the challenge of the hardforce there, and lurched on through. It was the familiar blue-white Continental owned by Tommy Carlotti, but there was something wrong about the way that car was moving. Tommy never drove a car that slowly in his whole life. Either something was wrong with the car—or something was wrong with Tommy—or that was *not* Tommy.

Vannaducci shrugged off his dressing gown, grabbed his suit jacket off the back of a chair, and hurried downstairs in his shirtsleeves.

He was standing in the entry hall and completing

31

his dressing when the door banged open and Ralph Pepsi, the watch captain, came charging in.

"What's up?" Vannaducci asked in a voice that did not quite conceal the vague uneasiness lurking there.

"It's Mr. Carlotti, here finally. But he's got a problem. He wants Johnny Powder out there double quick."

The *capo* snapped his head to the side and growled, "Then you better get him."

The guard captain hurried off toward the back of the house. Vanaducci stepped outside just as Frank Ebo, the house boss, was starting down the broad steps to the portico. The Continental was pulled to the curb down there, and the strained, unhappy face of Tommy Carlotti was visible through the front window.

Frank Ebo was a big man with a perpetually red face and worried expression—a total pessimist who saw invisible feds behind every tree and nonexistent bugs in every telephone and flower vase. But he was a good house boss, a comfort to have around. It was Ebo's job to be worried.

He was skirting around the front of Carlotti's vehicle, where he paused to kick a tire, then he drew back as though seeking a different angle of vision. He was not looking at the tire, though, as he called out, "G'morning, Tom. Problem with the car?"

"No it's fine, the car's fine," Carlotti replied in a curiously flattened voice. "Except the damn thing is going to blow up any minute."

Ebo chuckled, then stiffened and asked, "You serious?"

"You don't see me laughing, do you?"

32

"Then get the hell out of it!"

"Can't. Guy says it's a dead man's trigger. Soon's I let go—blooey! What the hell'm I gonna do, Frank?"

"Can you drive it?"

" 'Course I can *drive* it. I drove it the hell *in* here, didn't I?"

"Then drive it the hell *out!*"

"F'God's sake, Frank! I came for help!"

"You'll get it, but not here at the front door! Drive it out!"

"Where to?" Carlotti asked in a defeated voice.

"Well, shit, anywhere! Take it out on the grass—*way* out on the grass!"

"You don't know what I'm going through!" the tortured man yelled. "My fuckin' foot's going *numb*, I'm tellin' you! One little slip, Frank, and . . ."

Vannaducci intervened at that point, calling down, "You gonna be okay, Tommy boy. Johnny Powder's coming. Now you do like Frank tells you. Frank, lead the way. Take 'im out there in the oval by the hedges. Tommy—you just follow Frank, slow'n easy though."

An overwrought Ebo called back, "You shouldn't be out here, Marco. Maybe you should go back inside."

"Maybe you oughtta let Marco decide where Marco oughtta be," the old man retorted. "Go on now and do what I said!"

The house boss pivoted about and strode quickly along the drive and onto the lawn, calling heated instructions to unseen hardmen as he did so. "Stay clear of that car! It's got a bomb! Alfie and Herm, stick to Mr. Vannaducci! Two of you boys run down to the gate and back up that crew, but stay outta

33

sight! This could be a trick, so let's watch it! Alla you boys keep moving, don't just stand around! Eyes and ears open!"

He guided the threatening vehicle to a position on the front lawn about fifty yards from the house.

Vannaducci descended to the yard and followed at a discreet distance with a couple of Ebo's men falling in, a step behind, at each elbow. Other men were straggling from the house, attracted by all the commotion. In that group were Harry Scarbo, Vannaducci's man across the river in Algiers; Rocco Lanza, the financial go-between for many of Vannaducci's semilegit activities; and strongman Enrico Campenaro, chief enforcer for the entire empire.

Johnny Powder, an explosives expert, was in the rear but moving up quickly, in shirtsleeves and carrying a toolbox.

Out on the lawn, Frank Ebo was maintaining a respectful distance from the vehicle, now safely distanced from the house. "What kind of bomb, Tom?" he asked, as though merely hoping to keep the other man's mind busy.

"Hell, I don't . . ."

"What's it look like? I mean, the gadget—the thing you're holding."

"I'm not holding anything. I'm holding it *down*. Just a box, a little box. About six inches square. Maybe three inches thick. Stuck to the floor beside the brake pedal. There's a button on top, a metal thingamajig. The guy armed it, and said I had fifteen seconds to get that button down and *keep* it down."

"What guy?"

"*What* guy! Jesus Christ, you don't even know *what guy?*" Carlotti was obviously falling apart

34

quickly—the voice shrill, shaky. "Some mortgage *that* is, some fancy goddam . . . listen, Frank . . . now, listen! My foot's getting numb. I can't even feel the damned thing, and my leg is shaking off. You get somebody out here quick that can do something more'n ask dumb questions!"

"He's coming, Tommy. Take it easy. He's coming. Listen. Bend down and try rubbing the foot. Keep the blood circulating. Or stomp it with your other foot. Keep the pressure on that way."

"I'm not stomping nothing," Carlotti growled raggedly, but obviously more composed now. His head disappeared from view.

Vannaducci, listening to all this from a safe distance, moved to intercept Johnny Powder. He grabbed his arm and gazed somberly into the bomber's eyes as he told him, "You get Tommy boy out of that jam, Johnny. None of us'll ever forget it."

The expert responded with a worried nod of the head and moved on.

The *capo* tailed along until he reached Ebo's position. The house boss briefed Johnny Powder on the situation, then asked him, "Does that sound straight to you?"

"Sure," the bomber replied casually. "Simple circuit breaker. Little insulated plunger goes down between the contacts. Spring-loaded gadget. Release it and you get contact. Get contact, and you get a big boom."

"We don't want none of those," Vannaducci interjected.

Ebo asked, "He wouldn't have time to release it and scramble out of there?"

"I couldn't say that for sure. Prob'ly not. That's, uh, Tommy Carlotti in there?"

"Yeah. And going to pieces fast. You may not have much time, Johnny."

"What's he doing? I don't even see him."

"I think he's trying to hold the foot down with his hands. Says his leg's shaking, foot's numb. Wouldn't even knew if his foot slipped off."

"He'd know," Johnny Powder said. "We'd all know." He shot a troubled glance at Vannaducci.

"What can you do?" the old man asked.

"Depends. We might both get blown up. But . . ." The bomber lit a cigarette, took a deep drag, dropped it and put it out on the grass, and sauntered to the vehicle—calmly calling out, "Okay, Mr. Carlotti, just keep that plunger engaged."

Carlotti's strained face appeared at the window. "The—my leg's jumping like crazy," he reported. "I'm trying to hold it steady."

"You'd better. Can you reach the plunger with your hands?"

"No. The damn steering wheel . . ."

"I'm going to open the door. Now don't let go. Keep that thing engaged. We'll be laughing at this tomorrow over a couple of sweating broads. Eh? Right?"

Carlotti managed a nervous cackle and replied, "You're my man, Johnny. Anything you say."

"Then I say it's hot broads tomorrow, for both of us."

Johnny Powder was on his knees and leaning into the vehicle with head and shoulders inside, tool kit on the ground beside him. After a moment he told Carlotti, "Okay, I got it, but wait a minute now, don't relax yet. Don't move till I tell you to. See, here's where we are now. I got a clamp on the shoe. But there's not much sole there to hang onto—that's really not much of a shoe, Mr. Carlotti. It could slip loose if we're not careful. Here's what, now. I'm going to unbuckle the shoe. When I say, you slip your foot out, but do it real easy. I mean, don't move that shoe a hair, not a hair."

"God, it's numb. I can't even feel . . ."

"I'll help. Here we go now. Come on . . . easy . . . *eee-zy*." The bomber let out a long sigh. "Okay. It's broads tomorrow, Mr. Carlotti."

Then the underboss was tumbling from the car onto hands and knees in the grass, crawling vigorously for safe distance. Ebo ran forward to grab his arm and pull him along.

Johnny Powder remained at his post, kneeling in the open doorway.

Scarbo, Lanza, and Campenaro had joined their *capo* at the edge of danger.

Carlotti was sprawled on his back at Vannaducci's feet, gulping air and trembling with the release of tension. Ebo, kneeling beside the rescued underboss, asked him, "How'd you get in a mess like that?"

Before Carlotti could find breath enough to reply, the bomb expert's muffled yelp announced from the vehicle, "Something's funny here! It's got another—"

Something in there popped and sizzled. Johnny Powder flung himself out of there backwards and rolled across the lawn at the same instant that a muffled miniature explosion at the rear of the vehicle puffed open the trunk hood and sent both rear doors askew and gaping.

Ebo had instinctively gone to full prone alongside Tommy Carlotti and brought Vannaducci tumbling beside him. The other bosses quickly followed suit; enforcer Campenaro hit the ground with a gun in his paw.

Johnny Powder, alive and apparently well in the grass, gasped, "Wise bastard! Had another gadget on the bottom of the box. Soon as I moved it . . ."

Vannaducci growled, "What the hell is it, then? Is that all it's gonna do now?"

The bomb man lurched to his feet and grimly closed on the problem once again. Gingerly he peered into the rear-seat area, then shot a glance toward the congregation of men kneeling in the safe zone, and went on to check out the trunk compartment. He straightened almost immediately from that inspection and called over, "Yeah, that's all. I guess it's all he wanted to do. I guess this is for you, Mr. Vannaducci—you'll have to come see for yourself. It's safe now, no more surprises."

"Come see what?" the *capo* growled nervously, but he was already moving forward. The others trailed out in his wake and fanned around beside him at the open trunk compartment of Tommy Carlotti's lightly damaged car.

Johnny Powder muttered, "Charges were on the locks, see. Clean job, very clean. The guy could've had any effect he wanted."

But it was not the clean job that captured the attention of the assembly of bosses. It was the cargo. A corpse lay curled in that compartment. A big chunk of the forehead was missing, and what was left was pretty messy, but there was no mistaking the remains of Big Ed Latina, the boss of western Louisiana.

"What's this, what's this?" Carlotti mumbled, dazed. "I didn't know about this."

Someone said, "There's another one on the floor, back seat."

"It's Skipper Watson," another lowered voice reported. Watson had been a Vannaducci front for offshore oil interests.

"So now we're all here," Vannaducci commented, his mood mixed with anger and sorrow.

"I didn't know about the Skipper and Big Ed," Carlotti insisted quietly. "But Scooter and his boys are gone, too. All of them, same way. Marco . . . it was Mack Bolan. He did this, all of this."

The old man pried a marksman's medal from Big Ed's fist, bounced it once on his palm, and passed it on to Campenaro. "So, it's true," the *capo* said gloomily. "And this boy moves fast. Listen. All of you, listen. This is why I called the parley. Somebody hit our bank run this morning, over on the Pearlington cutoff. Jimmy Lista might live and he might not. All his boys are dead."

Silence descended on the group like a heavy pall. Johnny Powder slowly closed the trunk hood and leaned on it to keep it down. One of the underbosses lit a cigar; another spat in his hands and rubbed it in.

Frank Ebo was the one to break the silence. Though not an underboss in the true sense of the word, he held rank here by virtue of his supreme responsibility for the *capo's* skin. "I don't like it, Tommy coming in here wired this way. He led the guy right here, Marco. It was a bad move."

39

"Aw, bullshit," Carlotti said in a flat, dispirited voice. "That son of a bitch didn't need me to lead him anywhere. Listen. He knows all of us, everything about us. He just used me as a messenger boy. Imagine that. Using *me* as a messenger."

"Some message," someone grunted.

"You better count your blessings, Tommy," another boss suggested.

Indeed, that seemed to be the mood now pervading the entire gathering. As for the "message" itself —it was one that needed no elaboration, delivered in a manner most certain to be fully understood by this particular gathering of men.

Vannaducci sighed and told his group, "We better get inside and talk about this. This boy moves fast, and I think we got ourselves real trouble this time."

Yes, there was big trouble in River City. But it was only the beginning, and all the king's men knew that truth without the smallest reservation. On the eve of Mardi Gras, the Executioner's war had reached the Golden Empire.

If, however, there had been any lingering doubts on that score, they were to be immediately dispelled.

Richard Zeno, *consigliere* to the Vannaducci Family, was hurrying across the lawn toward the group.

"Marco," he called breathlessly ahead. "Just got word from town. They say Mack Bolan's running wild in the French Quarter. He's hit Toby Never's place, Joe DelMonico's, and Marty Jackson's Jazz Joint. All hell's breaking loose over there!"

Yes. For everyone at that gathering, the Executioner's message was loud and clear. And here was a "boy" who would not be impressed by tribute from the broker.

5: CO-OPTED

Literally translated from the Latin, the word "carnival" means "farewell to meat." In Roman Catholic tradition, Carnival commences on the twelfth night after Christmas and reaches its climax on Shrove Tuesday, the day of feasting before Ash Wednesday, the first day of Lent.

As celebrated in the city of New Orleans, the tradition actually has closer links to Pagan Rome and the bacchanalian orgies of that period.

Though there is much pomp and memorable splendor to the official activities of a New Orleans Mardi Gras—with parades and formal costume balls, the crowning of kings and queens, organized events and celebrations spanning a two-week period—the big climax is on Fat Tuesday, and the real action for the million or so visitors is to be found in the streets of the French Quarter, which, at such times, has been described as "the world's largest insane asylum." It is no place for the faint-hearted or weak-minded. Vehicular traffic is barred from the district, except for official and emergency vehicles. Mounted policemen appear as small and isolated islands of purely symbolic security in the surging waves of humanity sweeping those streets, and even the cops sometimes flip out and become one with the giddy sea of revelers.

It is impossible to preserve order under such conditions, even though every cop and auxiliary at the city's command is pressed into the situation. This thought was occupying the gloomy consciousness of Lieutenant Jack Petro as he sat at the conference table with his peers in city hall and listened to the reading of reports on the newest thing in Mardi Gras —a new King Carnival, as it were—the impossible, the unbelievable, the spectacular Mack Bolan and his series of punches to the city's groin that were threatening to outweigh all other worries in the official mind.

The mayor was greatly upset, and understandably so. "Why *now?*" he kept asking. "Why is this guy doing this *now?*—at a time like *this?*"

It was a purely rhetorical question, of course— born of official anguish and desperation. Actually, what better time for a guy like Bolan to invade New Orleans? From his point of view, naturally. With nearly a million visitors on hand and thousands more arriving every hour, all with nothing to do but churn aimlessly through the city, choke the public facilities, sing and dance and get drunk in the streets, jam the jails and the hospitals—the police couldn't even guarantee the visitors safety from one another. How could they possibly even

43

hope to cope with a guy like Mack Bolan running wild through that insanity?

A standing joke among the cops was the probably imaginative but entirely possible story of the lady from Omaha who one year was had five times in a crowd on the corner of Bourbon and Toulouse, without once leaving her feet and with no idea whatever of who was tapping her at any given moment. She hadn't missed a Mardi Gras since—or so the story went. The true stories that wound up on the official police blotter—and these probably represented a small fraction of the total crimes—were much less humorous and were often tragic. There was no way to effectively police a Mardi Gras.

And now the big Mack was adding his imposing weight to the problem. There would be blood flowing with the whiskey and wine, gunshots mingling with the cries of merriment, and a lot of hot corpses to serve up in the "farewell to meat."

Some farewell!

Some Mardi Gras!

Petro forced his mind back to the oral reading of too-familiar reports. Barely eight o'clock of the morning and already the guy'd had a busy day. He'd knocked over an armored truck and gotten away clean with about $400,000, killing fourteen men in the process and critically wounding another. Then he'd sashayed into the French Quarter to bust Carlotti's palace on Royal Street. Known dead there: five. Carlotti himself missing. Next he'd taken a walking tour of Bourbon Street and closed three of the most troublesome dives in the city. None dead in that foray, but a lot of property damage and some damned well terrified people. It was rumored that

Joe DelMonico, whose B-girl clipjoint was one of those hit, was frantically seeking air transportation out of the country. Toby Never's private club, a bar and whorehouse on lower Bourbon, was mysteriously emptied of patrons and employees in the early postdawn and was now decorated with "Closed for Mardi Gras" signs—on a street where *nothing* closed *ever* and especially not during Carnival. Marty Jackson's Jazz Joint, a long-suspected "powder house" for street pushers, was similarly shuttered; reliable informants reported that the proprietor—known on the street as "Acid Malloy"—had checked into a local hospital for "tests and rest," and that all of Malloy's stock for Mardi Gras had been torched.

Yeah. A busy guy. In a busy town.

Petro's mind was wandering again—and it was just as well when the clerk stepped behind his chair to whisper into his ear, "Lieutenant, there's an urgent call for you. A male, Northern accent. Won't identify himself but insists it's urgent and can't wait."

The rackets specialist gladly accepted the excuse to duck out of Morning Reports. He quietly followed the clerk to the anteroom, leaned against the wall while lighting a cigarette, then picked up the indicated line.

"Petro here," he announced.

A pleasant male voice inquired, "This the same Petro who testified at the congressional hearings a while back?"

"Guilty," the lieutenant replied. "What's urgent? Who's this?"

"This is Bolan."

"Who?"

45

"Mack Bolan."

Petro snatched the cigarette from his mouth and jabbed it in the direction of the clerk, then made a sign with his fingers. The guy nodded and poked a button on the base of the control instrument.

Petro growled into the phone, "Come on, don't piss me around. I don't have time for Carnival gags."

"Believe it or don't, Petro, but stay on. I understand you're the department liaison with the New Orleans Crime Commission. That still hold?"

"Right. Uh, what's this I hear about Acid Malloy? If you're who you say, then you should know all—"

"There was a shipment for Malloy in the armored car I hit this morning. Came in on the Villa Merchant at Gulfport last night. Fifty kilos, uncut. I delivered it, tied to a magnesium stick. The shock was too much for Malloy. He decided to take a rest."

"What happened to Tommy Carlotti?"

"He went to the farm." A dry chuckle. "With a very heavy foot."

"What's that mean?"

"Ask him. He's still out there with Marco and what's left of the cadre. Strategy meeting."

"And Scooter Favia?"

"He tried too hard. Had to punch him. You satisfied now?"

The clerk was giving Petro a negative signal, which meant the call was probably nontraceable. Petro told his caller, "Maybe. What'd you want from me?"

"Information."

"Go to hell!" the cop snorted.

"Okay. But your town could go there with me. You could save a little. I have a trade for you."

46

"What're you trading?" the lieutenant asked in a milder tone.

"Some intelligence your crime commission has been digging for these past few years. Books, ledgers, records—the whole interconnecting network of Vannaducci's money outlets in the legit community."

"Where'd you get all that?"

Another dry chuckle. "Let's say I inherited it."

"How long you been in this town, Bolan?"

"Long enough. I have their numbers now. I'm aiming for a clean sweep. In case I stub my toe along the way, though . . . well, I think you should have this information."

"And what do you want from me?"

"Someone is doing a hell of a sweet job of electronic surveillance on the money man, Rocco Lanza. It's not feds, and it's not local cops. I need to know if that crime commission is running the exercise."

Petro hesitated, then said, "Why do you need to know?"

"Just believe that I do. And that the knowledge could save a lot of ruckus. Look, Petro, I don't like busting your town. Especially at a time like this. I'd like to get it over with as quickly and painlessly as possible. What about this surveillance?"

"What's so important about that?"

"It's damned important."

"How, uh, how do you know it's not a police operation?"

The guy chuckled again, but it wasn't so pleasant this time—more like ice cubes clinking into a metal basin. "I remain alive by knowing things like that, Petro."

47

"You think maybe Marco is bugging his own people?"

"I've entertained the idea. There are other possibilities."

"Like what?"

"Like maybe some of the *amici* up north are bugging Marco."

Petro paused to think about that briefly, then he sighed and said, "Well maybe you're right about that."

"Thanks, I'll take that as an answer to my question. You'll receive my part of the deal by special messenger. It's already on the way."

"Yeah, sure it is."

"You can believe it," the cool voice assured him. "No reason for me to con you."

"Bolan, wait! You still there?"

"I'm here."

"Look, man, you're right, it is a bad time in New Orleans. We got nearly a million civilians jamming this town right now. So go away. What the hell do you think cops are for? We'll clean up our own."

"How long have you had Mafia in your town, Petro? You're not old enough to remember back that far. Your father isn't old enough."

"We're working on it," the lieutenant said, bristling.

"No way your way. I know it and you know it. It's like trying to cure cancer with aspirins. Eases the pain a little now and then, but your vital tissue keeps disappearing."

Petro snapped, "You'll get no quarter in this town, Bolan! You'll be shot on sight!"

48

"I haven't asked for quarter. If you see me, Petro, bang away."

"Look, dammit—Bolan, wait, don't hang up! Damn the—okay, okay! I won't bullshit you, guy. Most of the cops in this town would rather shake your hand than slap leather on you. Unofficially, of course. The others are probably on the take and scared to death you'll upset their plans for early retirement. None of that's the point, though. Look—you're a decent guy, I buy that. You've never shot a cop, and I'd almost bet my life that you never will. That's not the point, either. The point is that there's a million civilian visitors in this town and more pouring in every hour. They're half nuts already. You start gunplay in the streets, and a thousand will get trampled in the panic. You've just—aw, hell, it's no good with a telephone between us. Let's meet. You say when and where. You have my word I'll be clean."

The guy's voice softened to near warmth as he said, "You're a good cop, Petro. I knew that before I called you. But I can't meet you. There'd be no point to it, anyway. Don't worry about your Carnival. There'll be no gunplay in the streets."

"Wait, dammit—"

"Sorry. Thanks for the cooperation. Stay hard, cop."

Petro found himself spluttering into a buzzing disconnect.

"Well, I'll be damned," he quietly told the police clerk.

"I got it on tape," the clerk said. "What do you want me to do with it?"

"Play it for Morning Reports," Petro muttered.

"Next week." He pushed himself away from the desk, took a dazed step toward the conference room, then spun around and headed for the ready room to await his surprise package from the new King Carnival.

6: TRACKED

It was still a few hours before noon when Bolan returned to an exhaustively scouted zone on the southern shore of Lake Pontchartrain, well removed from Mardi Gras madness—an upper-middle class neighborhood not far from the New Orleans campus of Louisiana State University.

Rocco Lanza kept quarters there in an immodest split-level palace featuring bulletproof glass, covered pool-patio with same, and had sentry dogs roaming loose about the grounds, which jutted into the lake with water on three sides.

Lanza was perhaps the single, most important cog in Vannaducci's crime cartel. It was through the financier that the unimaginable millions of black bucks illegally siphoned from the economy of the South each year found their way back into the same economy in a clouded maze of clandestine investments that could only make the rich richer and the poor much, much poorer.

Bolan had been interested in Lanza from the beginning of this Southern expedition—and it had been a mere stroke of luck that turned the Executioner on to the fact that he was not the only one "scouting" the Pontchartrain headshed of locally syndicated business-crime.

It had started as a daring intelligence mission, with Bolan probing various angles and approaches for effective electronic surveillance. He'd gone in soft on a clouded night with tranquilizer darts for the dogs, and he'd sectored the whole place, stood in every room, explored the basement and the roof and the outbuildings—even the bottom of the pool —and he'd set up his gadgets for automatic collection of intelligence.

With all that, it was not until two days later that he discovered that he was not the only one collecting data from Rocco Lanza. He'd accidentally punched in the wrong crystal while setting up a standby receiver, and the recorder began whirring away before he could correct the error. On time-scaled playback, the signal was weak and wavery, but the voice was unmistakably Lanza's. The weak signal, he deduced, was caused by the fact that the miniature transmitters required for such work depended on precision beaming of the microwaves to the receiving station. Bolan had evidently blundered into a fringe area of reception.

Then it had required several days of patient monitoring with a mobile receiver for Bolan to catch and track the quick-pulse transmissions, to draw a line-of-sight zone of probability between illicit transmitter and hidden receiver—but still he had caught no glimpse of the "scout" and could only surmise the probable point of reception.

On this visit, on the day the blitz began, Bolan came armed with a theodolite for precision visual sighting. And he came in a rented boat. He also came in time for the morning broadcast of purloined information. He positioned himself across the probability line, receiver and theodolite ready, and he got his sighting.

The sober face became creased in an appreciative grin as he translated his reading into the focal field of powerful binoculars and immediately zeroed-in on the clandestine transmitter.

And, sure, it was cute. Damned cute. A small package no more than four inches square, piggy-backing the rotor motor on the television antenna atop the Lanza place, inconspicuous to a fault and broadcasting a pencil beam of intelligence in quick-pulse playback from probably a dozen miniature recorders stashed about that joint. Better than Bolan's arrangement, for sure. And Bolan had learned from the best.

It appeared to be a spanking new television antenna set-up, and it was easy to speculate on the fate of an earlier one and the machinations required to place just the right guy in just the right time and place to provide the new installation—as modified, of course, to suit the installer.

The thought brought a smile to Bolan's face as he swiveled 180 degrees to follow the downrange leg of the beam. Another boat, about a mile out, loomed into the vision field of the binoculars—a mahogany inboard runabout, again inconspicuous on the huge lake that stretched more than twenty-five miles northward.

The Executioner donned a yachting cap and kicked his big cruiser onto a 360 course. This was going to be interesting. Also, it could turn out to be highly significant to the Southern campaign.

It did.

Bolan's sudden move had been spotted, as he'd expected it would, but there was to be no contest between the two craft. The runabout leapt off its mark almost immediately, swinging northeastward on an evasive course, but the water was choppy out there, and the smaller boat was running against the wind and waves.

The cruiser gained steadily. In a matter of seconds, Bolan's binoculars were focusing on the profile of a beautiful but frightened young woman—the only occupant of the open two-seater. Bolan's jaw tightened as he released the glasses and continued closing.

He overtook the quarry in open water and a long way from anywhere, and he could see the desperate whites of her eyes as he raised the big silver Auto Mag and gave her a look at it.

The girl's shoulders slumped forward, and she killed the power, staring the pursuer down for a moment, then dropping the gaze in defeat.

He circled her once as the little boat lost headway, then he came in on her quarter and tied the boats together.

"Come aboard," he commanded.

"What's this all about?" she yelled back, eyes jerking angrily as she stood up for the transfer.

He gave her a hand and pulled her aboard the

cruiser. A small girl—maybe a hundred pounds if dipped in egg yolk and rolled in bread crumbs—well made and beautifully proportioned, wind whipping at the silken jacket and pressing white flared slacks into the background of curvaceous thighs—luminous eyes that could reflect fear and anger with gloom and excitement, all at once—a beauty, a vaguely familiar brazen beauty, and the very last thing Mack Bolan needed in his life in this time and circumstance.

She hit the deck of the cruiser with a flounce and took a swing at him.

He caught the tiny fist and pressed a marksman's medal into it, by way of introduction.

"Easy," he told her. "We could be friends or enemies."

She did a blank double take from the bull's-eye cross to a roving search of that granite face, then she reacted.

"Ohhh!" she cried. "Oh, thank God! Thank God for miracles!"

Bolan showed the girl a sober smile and told her, "I guess that means we're friends."

"My name is Toni Blancanales," she puffed, "and you'd better damn well *know* we're friends!"

Friends, indeed.

The Executioner had tracked a potential enemy scout and caught the kid sister of his old buddy and Death Squad survivor, Rosario "the Politician" Blancanales.

And now he knew who'd engineered the fantastically sophisticated eavesdrop on Rocco Lanza. It could be none other than Gadgets Schwarz, the other surviving Death Squadsman.

But why? For whom? What the hell were Pol and Gadgets doing mixing in the battle for New Orleans?

More, still, what sort of unhappy situation could have possibly induced Pol to bring his kid sister in on such a hazardous operation?

The answers to that would, to be sure, prove highly significant to the Southern campaign.

7: DOUBLE TAKE

The Death Squad had been formed during an early period of the Executioner's war on organized crime. Hastily assembled in Los Angeles shortly after the first pitched battle of Bolan's war effort, the nine members came from diverse backgrounds and brought unique talents to the squad. They had little in common except the Vietnam war, their interrelated part in it, a similar fate as veterans of it, and their misfit status as men competent at war but now psychologically suited for little else.

Each of the squad had found realization of self in the high attainment of the grimmest skill of all: expertise at death and destruction. Which is not to say that the Death Squad was composed of bloodthirsty war merchants; it was simply that postwar life was anticlimactic and flat for these men who were on the high, dramatic edge of "life on the heartbeat."

Each of them had gladly dropped the humdrum

that was "life after Vietnam" and rallied to the Executioner's call.

Another thing they held in common was an unshakable respect and admiration for Mack Bolan, and he for them.

He knew now that the squad had been ill-conceived and unwisely fielded. They had understood the high-risk factors of their game, of course, and certainly all were as aware as Bolan that they could not continue indefinitely against the impossible odds confronting them. Still, Bolan blamed himself for bringing them into his problem—and he felt heavily the burden of responsibility for the deaths of seven of the greatest guys to ever walk his warpaths.

Only Blancanales and Schwarz survived that climactic death charge on the DiGeorge Family of Southern California, and even they had gone to jail. Thanks to Bolan's "war purse," some great legal talent, and a sympathetic state prosecutor, Pol and Gadgets had been allowed to plead to misdemeanor charges and had spent very little time behind bars. They were marked men from that day, however—marked by the mob for death—and their lives had become a dismal charade of hiding behind assumed identities and depressingly low-profile life styles.

As for the dead seven, Bolan would forever carry them in his heart and conscience, and that traumatic experience in Los Angeles would always affect his decisions in war and the question of "taking on allies." He had worked alone ever since, except for a bit of indirect assistance now and then from old friends and new who seemed somehow destined to keep cropping up on his paths of war.

There had been a single exception to the "man alone" routine, and that had been in San Diego—quite a few battles back—and the exception had been, sure, Blancanales and Schwarz once again. Bolan had, in fact, been summoned to San Diego by the two on a rescue mission for a former C.O. The San Diego siege had its bad memories too—but not any involving the two Death Squad survivors. They'd come through that one with not only physical dimensions well intact but with new horizons for their personal lives as well. At their farewell in San Diego, Bolan had suggested that the two pool their unique talents and go into a business befitting those talents—and again Bolan had donated his war purse to get them started.

The Executioner war had been a hot one ever since—with a lot of miles, blood, and corpses separating San Diego from New Orleans—and there'd been no further contact between Bolan and his buddies from Able Team. He hadn't even known if they had actually established their private enterprise, or even if they'd remained in the country.

Now he knew.

The story spilling from Toni Blancanales during that tense return to the yacht harbor confirmed that the men had indeed formed their company—an investigations outfit called "Able Group"—and that they had come to New Orleans "on a job."

According to the girl, Able Group did not handle illegal assignments. They specialized in electronic security—a sort of counterespionage service for small companies and professional men who, for one reason or another, might themselves be subjected to illegal surveillance.

And things had been going pretty well. Toni considered it a sign of the times that such a service was in widespread demand.

Able Group had come to Louisiana in response to a one-shot contract with a political headquarters upstate. The politicos wondered if they were being bugged. Able Group confirmed the suspicion, neutralized the problem, and instructed the locals in basic security and detection routines. That contract led to another small job, this one in Baton Rouge, and it was there that they were approached by a "Mr. Kirk" who presented credentials that identified him with the governor's office.

Mr. Kirk had a special hush-hush job for Able Group. He provided them with a written contract, an electronic surveillance authorization carrying the purported signature and seal of a U. S. district judge, and apparently the full backing of the state of Louisiana.

The job: bug Rocco Lanza.

Neither of the partners had ever heard of Lanza. The background story given by Mr. Kirk seemed plausible enough. The official documents appeared genuine. Still, they had misgivings about accepting the job—something had seemed off center.

It bothered both men that they were forbade contacts with state police or other governmental agents; Kirk was to be their only point of contact. Their fees and expenses were paid in cash from a special fund, which, Kirk hinted, was partially subsidized by Washington.

Kirk partly allayed their vague worries with an enigmatic story about "political interconnections in the police establishment" and "the need for absolute secrecy until we're ready to indict."

It was their first big job—Able Group took it, misgivings and all.

It had then required two weeks to set the thing up, to get inside that house on the point, plant their equipment, then actually institute surveillance.

They had beaten Mack Bolan to the job by three days.

Neither man had been seen or heard from since.

Toni Blancanales was half out of her mind with worry. She was an "agent" for Able Group as well as secretary and business manager. Usually she participated in the planning and setup phases, doing her thing as a "cheesecake decoy" and con girl. It was she who had "sold" Rocco Lanza the new TV antenna installation, including wall-jacks in every room of the house, even the bathrooms.

"I've sold everything from bibles to condominiums," she told Bolan. "It's no harder to sell bugs."

Bolan could believe it. She was quite a gal. Not quite the "kid" he'd thought, either. She looked eighteen but was closer to twenty-five, a third-year dropout from Columbia—worked briefly as an airline stewardess, from there married and divorced ("almost overnight—he was a rat")—from that moment on almost as restless as her brother, whom she called "Rosie."

Toni had jumped at the offer to join Able Group and now regarded her role there as "my niche in life."

Niche or not, she was a very distraught young

61

lady when Mack Bolan made his personal appearance into her life.

"It's just not like the boys to go off and not keep in touch," she said dismally. "I know something's gone sour, I know it has."

She had not been able to locate Mr. Kirk or anyone who would even admit to knowing him. The writ authorizing the electronic surveillance did not check out; it was a forgery. Toni had checked all the jails, morgues, and hospitals in the area.

Finally, in desperation, she'd returned to "the scene of the crime"—the Lanza place, on the pretext of a customer-satisfaction check, only to find "everyone charming" and "no bad vibes" to indicate an awareness of the dirty work in the antenna job.

"So this morning I took the boat out to the drop to see if the thing was still operational. It was." She held up the tape with a rueful smile. "As far as I know, this is only the second collection. The last I saw of Rosie and Gadgets, they were headed out here for the first pickup. That was a week ago. It was supposed to be a proof run, a check of the technical quality. If all was okay, they were to then contact Mr. Kirk and turnkey the whole works to him. Our job was done."

"But you never heard from them," Bolan commented. "You don't know that they actually made a pickup, or that they ever contacted this guy Kirk."

"Right. And Mr. Kirk has become a wraith. I would have to wonder if he ever existed, except that I saw him once."

"You *saw* him?"

"Yes. At the last meeting to seal the deal. It was

62

at Marty Jackson's Jazz Joint, a dive on Bourbon Street."

Bolan's hackles quivered.

"What's the matter?" she asked, noting the flash of Executioner eyes.

"Nothing. Go on."

"That's all. Kirk didn't see *me*, if that's what's bothering you. At least, not in any reference to Rosie and Gadgets. I was at the bar, looking as demure as possible, while the boys met with Kirk at a back table. I was sort of—sort of . . ."

"Scouting the backtrack," Bolan suggested.

"Yes. We sometimes do that. Gadgets calls it 'double-teaming'—he's very security conscious."

"A lesson hard learned in Vietnam," Bolan said with a tight smile. "Can you describe this man Kirk?"

"Better than that," she replied. "He has a famous look-alike."

The hackles stood stiffly to attention and Bolan growled, "Yeah?"

"Yeah," she said, mimicking his tone. "You know the dreamboat Italian singer, Enzo Stuarti?"

Bolan turned his face away from that revelation, not wanting the girl to see the certain conclusion in his eyes, nor the ghosts from the past swirling through his consciousness.

At the moment he would not have given a marksman's medal for the chance that Gadgets Schwarz and Rosario Blancanales would ever be seen or heard from again. The Death Squad, it seemed, was finally gone forever.

8: DOUBLE-TEAMED

There was no doubt in Bolan's mind that Tommy Carlotti was "Mr. Kirk"—the man behind the mysterious surveillance of Rocco Lanza. The major question remaining unanswered was the one of motivation. Was Carlotti carrying the action on his own? Was he doing it under orders from Marco Vannaducci? Or was he working in collusion with some outside party?

It would be utter nonsense to even consider the possibility that the whole thing had been no more than a snare for Blancanales and Schwarz. There would have been no need to go that far with such a scheme; if Carlotti or others in the mob had known the true identity of the pair, the first contact would have been the last—if that had been the logic behind the contact.

Bolan had returned both boats to the yacht harbor and docked them. He asked Toni, "Were the guys still using their cover names?"

She nodded. "Morales and Logan, yes. Rosie doesn't even introduce me as his sister, and I go by my married name—Davidson. Why? What are you thinking?"

He dismissed the far-out possibility with a shake of the head. "Nothing that would make sense. I was just wondering—you know, I guess, that there's an open Mafia contract on those two."

She replied, "Sure, I knew that. But what . . ."

"Don't you know yet that Lanza is a Mafia boss?"

The girl's eyelids fluttered rapidly over that idea.

Bolan hastily told her, "Relax, I've already dismissed the thing as a coincidence. Look, Toni—I'm running on damn tight numbers. That means that I'm into a blitz and I have to place every step with care. Do you know what I'm saying?"

She gave him a mechanical nod of the head.

She was one who always had it together, he was thinking. So lovely, so damned alluring—even while obviously worried and scared half out of her skull, she kept it together.

She was telling him, "You're about the closest thing to a god Rosie has ever believed in. Talks about you all the time." She showed Bolan a stiff smile. "Mack would do it this way—Mack did it that way. Yes, I know what you're saying. You're saying that Rosie and Gadgets can just go to hell, you've got a job to do."

He could not decide if she was working him, accusing him, or simply being outright candid. Pol had certainly thought the world of this kid sister. Carried wallet snapshots of her all through Vietnam, bragged about her constantly. "A chip off the old Blanc," he used to call her.

Bolan smiled sadly to himself and lit a cigarette while he thought into the situation. He blew the smoke toward the horizon upon which was perched the glass and stone mansion of Rocco Lanza, then quietly replied. "That's the way you see it, eh?"

"That's the way," she said. "It's also the way Pol would see it if your situations were reversed. You're both crazy. You put such importance on—on . . ."

Bolan was still gazing toward nowhere. Speaking almost to himself, he said, "I'd knock down the gates of hell if I thought I'd find them there. The problem is that I don't know. And I've already blown the soft approach. The mob knows I'm here, and they know I'm blitzing. The whole New Orleans mob is walking around on eggshells right now. Your man Kirk, by the way, is a local hood and budding *capo* by the name of Tommy Carlotti. I've already rousted him and put the mark of the beast on him. He'll be nowhere but in a crowd of torpedoes from here on."

"I'm sorry," the girl said quietly, dropping her gaze to an inspection of delicate hands—folding them, clasping them. "It's a fault of mine—leaping to judgment. You *are* concerned, aren't you?"

Bolan growled softly, "Sure I'm concerned. But you didn't let me finish stating the problem. There's more, and you may as well be aware of it. Time."

"What?"

"Time. Too much of it. Too little of it. You say they've been missing for a week. That's too damn long. Do you read that?"

Toni released a quivering breath as she replied, "Yes, I guess I read that."

"Okay. I'm going to do what I can. As I said, though, I'm on tight numbers. I'm committed to a timetable and a course of action that had all come together long before I knew about Able Group. I have to follow through on the battle plan. It's the only thing I can do at this stage of things. It's also probably the *best* thing I can do, as concerns Pol and Gadgets. If they're still alive—and I do mean *if* —then they're for sure in the hands of at least one of the factions I came here to bust. The best I can think to do at the moment is to simply bust on— and hope that our guys will get dislodged somewhere in the process."

Toni's lip curled as she commented, "Isn't that sort of like blowing up a burning building to save some people trapped on the top floor?"

"That's about what it amounts to," Bolan admitted. "But the whole town has gone hard by now, and that's the problem. Let me give you some background first, Toni, then I'm going to offer *you* a choice of action. Marco Vannaducci is the man and the power here. But he's old, dying slowly from a dozen ailments and plain decay, hounded by the feds—a desperate man desperately trying to hold together what he's got. And what he's got is an empire with annual revenues estimated at about a billion—that's a *billion*."

"That's a lot," Toni agreed, eyes saucered.

"More than the average person can even visualize. It's a lot of bucks and one hell of a magnetic attraction for a bunch of cutthroats who'd slash their bosom buddies for a handful of nickels. Marco's designated heirs are Carlotti, Lanza, and a few more psychopaths who each would love to be the only heir. And that's just one side of the coin. On the other are roughly a dozen other large Mafia families who control the rest of the country. They'd all love to get together and slice up this Southern pie for their own fat bellies. Are you reading?"

The girl had been watching him intently, studying him. "I was just thinking," she quietly admitted, "that Able Group sure stumbled into one hell of a mess."

"Right," Bolan agreed. "You did. But it wasn't carelessness that got you here. Vannaducci has the best-covered tracks in the country. It's layer upon layer of business fronts, concealed interests, the whole bit so interwoven and complicated that most of his own underbosses don't understand it. Except for Lanza. He's the business brain—and that's where the wicket gets sticky. There's a lot of local jealousy and maneuvering for position on the old man's inside track. At the moment, though, Lanza has the better track position because he's the only one who really understands the business. The others are hoods, street punks in the big time who got there by being the meanest on the block. Which doesn't make them the smartest—just the most dangerous. In one sense, they need Lanza. On the other hand, they're afraid he'll make the big grab and come up with all the goodies. So . . ."

"God, we really walked into it," Toni commented miserably.

"That still isn't all. I've been orchestrating a few things on my own. Setting it up, helping it mature, heating the pie and sending the odors wafting northward. The best way to beat a strong organization, especially a furtive one, is to get them to eating one another. I—"

"Divide and conquer."

"Right. Let the enemy engage itself. The pieces that are left are much easier to mop up. It's no coincidence of timing that I happen to be on the scene now, that I started my blitz when I did. I've been getting very strong intelligence readings of a crisis approaching for the Dixie mob, and timed for Mardi Gras. I rousted Carlotti this morning because I figured him for the strongest heir apparent, and I wanted to add some stiffening to his backbone."

"I don't understand that. Stiffened against what?"

"An invading coalition of New York and St. Louis mobs. It's been brewing a long time. St. Louis is the poorest territory in the country. It needs expansion. The New York bosses have decided it's time to stretch southward, before the old man lets everything fall to hell in intrafamily rivalry. St. Louis got the nod to move in. They've just been waiting for the right moment, and I believe this is it. I don't want them to find it too easy. I want a double knockout here—not an easy victory for either faction."

Toni said, "Wow. You're a sneaky dude, aren't you?"

"Name of the game," Bolan said. "I just want you to understand what I mean when I speak of tight numbers. And now we come to the nitty gritty. A course of action for you. What I'm going to suggest will carry an element of risk. Play it right, though, and I believe the risk will be minimal. How's your guts?"

"Shaking," she admitted with a droll smile. "But game. What's the suggestion?"

"Go to Lanza. Tell him the whole story—that is, about Kirk and the Able Group job. You've just discovered that your company was conned into an illegal surveillance contract, and your only wish now is to set things straight for the victim. Tell him how you conned him. Point out every bug in the place."

"Hey, wow," Toni said, ashen-faced. "He'll choke me and throw me in the pool. Won't he?"

"You conned him once, you could do it again. He liked you, didn't he?"

"Well, sure . . . but . . ."

"Play it right and cover yourself, you could come out with a friend for life. Consider the guy's position. He knows what's going on around him. You'll be doing him a big favor. You can show him his enemy. This Kirk guy, the one with a famous look-alike."

"He'd get that connection, eh?"

"He'd get it. Might even be inclined toward a bit of gallantry toward the lovely lady, help her spring her partners. That's the angle you have to play. Common friends against a common enemy. But— and this is important—you've never seen a tape from Lanza's house and you know absolutely *nothing* about his business matters. You're dumb, dumb, *dumb*—see?"

"That's easy," she commented shakily. "I just go in and be honest. Except I don't know he's Mafia."

"Right. You're scared, repentant, want to set things straight. And you want to find your partners."

She tossed her head and said, "Okay. I guess I can handle that. This will help your game, too, won't it?"

"It could," Bolan admitted. "It could also end yours—there's that possibility and you have to understand that. The whole thing could backfire. I'm

70

not urging you to do it. But if you want a course of action ..."

"What it sifts out to is 'put up or shut up.' Right?"

"That's not what I had in mind," Bolan assured her.

"It amounts to that, just the same. It's one thing to stamp one's foot and demand that somebody else *do* something. That's what I was doing, I guess. Now you're saying—"

"I'm saying nothing. It's a grasping at straws. I can't work an angle like that on Lanza. You can. If you want to." Bolan checked the time. "The meeting at Vannaducci's broke up an hour ago. Lanza will be home by now and digging fortifications. So I—"

"Where do you keep your crystal ball?" she asked, attempting a smile.

"I know my enemy," he explained. "First rule of warfare. Well—what do you say? Are you game for the game?"

"I'm game," she said, sighing. "But—how do we get back together? I mean, we *will*—won't we?"

"I'll try to cruise the corner of Claiborne and Canal at noon sharp, then at every even hour until we connect. I'll try, that's all I can promise."

"Fair enough. There's, uh, no place I can contact you by phone—or leave word?"

He grinned. "Not a chance. But if you just yell, from wherever you may happen to be, chances are I'll hear."

"You mean you've got this whole town wired for sound?"

"The pressure points, anyway."

"Gadgets told me once that you were a very apt pupil."

"I had a good teacher," Bolan replied, very sober once again. "Ready to push off?"

"Ready as I'll ever be," she said, trying and failing to be flippant.

He showed her a stern smile as he said, "Okay, hit the beach. Remember—it's *your* game. Stay hard."

"I know what that means, too," she told him. "First, though, I've got to *get* hard."

"You are," he assured her. "Toni . . ."

"Yes?"

"You're a hell of a gal."

"Thanks. You're a hell of a guy. *You* stay hard!"

She leapt to the pier and hurried away without looking back.

Bolan gave her a count of ten, then moved out behind her.

He wasn't about to let that kid go it alone—not for all the timetables in funnytown. But he was cooling it, laying back and scouting the backtrack, and it was just as well that no one knew that but himself—not even Toni.

The hardest lessons learned were the longest remembered.

Mack Bolan was security-conscious, too.

The Lanza joint would be double-teamed.

9: INSTRUMENT RANGE

Bolan's warwagon for the New Orleans operation was something new and special—a uniquely out fitted and beautifully integrated GMC motor home, a sleek low-profile 26-footer designed with the sportsman in mind. Bolan was no sportsman; for this warrior, the fabulous new vehicle represented a comfortably appointed mobile command post, a field headquarters, an armory, and electronics surveillance unit, all in one—it was base camp.

Most of the cost—about $100,000 of easy-come, easy-go Mafia-donated warchest funds—had been spent for special equipment and installation.

The electronics were courtesy of the space program and incorporated the most sophisticated developments of space-age science. A moonlighting NASA engineer provided the labor and materials for the basic radio gear. A technical genius from a local electronics firm did the rest, even to designing, building, and installing the computerlike selection and switching gear; highly sensitive directional audio pickup equipment; concealed or disguised antennae; optic marvels; a console for synchronizing, storing, sorting, editing, time-phasing, and even re-recording collected intelligence. He even had a mobile telephone and a simple radar unit.

The NASA engineer admiringly dubbed the completed project a "terran module," comparing it favorably with the best thing yet developed in lunar modules.

Bolan liked it, though he was a bit awed by the electronic capabilities of his new warwagon. It would have blown Gadgets Schwarz's electronic mind. What it all meant for Mack Bolan, in gross, was a wider range for his war effort. The gear in that van, of course, was entirely dependent on the military capabilities of the man it supported. He could "scan through" a neighborhood with the audio pickups operating and perhaps learn a thing or two about the enemy. He could probe for vehicles and unusual concealed masses of metal with the radar device. He could cruise within line-of-sight of planted radio bugs and trigger a quick-pulse collection without even stopping the vehicle—then unscramble, time-pulse, and play back the recording without leaving the driver's seat. But all these capabilities merely widened the scope for the warrior. They did not fight the battles.

Other special installations in the new warwagon provided the direct military support. There was a foldaway light-table for mapping and plotting battle lines, assault and withdrawal routes, and other tactical considerations. He had a fully equipped weapons lab and armory with concealed storage for munitions, explosives, tactical gadgets. In that lab he could build, modify, or repair all types of personal weapons as well as explosive devices.

Large picture windows along the sides were made of one-way glass, thus affording Bolan plenty of visibility while effectively shielding the interior from curious eyes.

Stock features on the vehicle included a 455-cubic-inch Toronado engine, slightly modified. Front traction with automatic transmission freed the rear tandem wheels from axles and conventional suspension—there were air bags instead of springs, adjustable from dashboard controls to raise or lower each side separately and compensate for uneven ground conditions. For animal comforts there was a galley, shower and toilet, and bunk space in the rear.

Completely self-contained, she was a warwagon in every sense and a long-needed complement to Bolan's war effort. Hopefully she would serve the man through many campaigns, but the sleek module would have been well worth the money if she carried him successfully through just this one.

Bolan was thinking, in fact, that she was worth it for the present task alone. He was parked at the lakeshore within view of the Lanza place—door open, a dummy fishing pole that was actually a mobile radio antenna clipped casually to the front bumper, Bolan himself seated in the comfortably padded high-backed console-type driver's seat and eyeing a reflecting plate installed at his right knee, part of the long-range optics capability.

Toni had been inside the joint for ten minutes. Bolan had heard her reception at the main entrance, thanks to the audio telescope—a sophisti-

75

cated "barrel mike." They'd tried to put her off. "Mr. Lanza" was "very busy" and couldn't be disturbed. Toni had tearfully insisted on an audience, Bolan grinning over her histrionics, which, at that, were about 95 percent genuine.

One of the hardmen finally came down to pass her through the dog defenses. At that moment, Bolan lost direct audio contact, but he'd tracked them across the grounds with the optics, then regained audio via radio implantation at the entry foyer.

Moving back to the switching gear at the electronics console, he'd tracked her through the house and into Lanza's private digs off the pool-patio area. It was a gruff greeting by the lord of the manse—a mood that changed rapidly to disbelief, anger, then anxiety as Toni spun the tale of betrayal and invasion of privacy.

At that point, Bolan had switched the audio monitoring to the front of the van and gone forward to maintain both visual and audio contact. He heard the breathless commands issuing from the inner sanctum, and moments later saw two hardmen running onto the grounds, heads craning toward the roof. Without benefit of barrel mikes he could hear the shout of discovery as one of the guys spotted the package atop the rotor control, then he watched with sober amusement as a ladder was brought around and a guy climbed hastily to the paydirt. Meanwhile not a word was coming through the radio pickup; Bolan understood this also—the sudden awareness of listening devices on the premises turns many normally garrulous people into mutes.

The guy on the roof tossed the package into a pair of waiting hands on the ground.

A moment later Bolan's speaker stirred with the sound of a door opening and closing, footsteps and harsh breathing, a clump as a solid object came to rest on a desktop—then Toni's quavery tones, "That's it. It's okay, you can talk now. That's the central collector and transmitter. Nothing can go out now."

Lanza's voice: "I'm a son of a bitch—pardon me, ma'am. I can't believe it! This little thing here can bug my whole house?"

Toni, explaining: "The actual bugs are in the antenna jacks, emplaced throughout the house. But they're harmless now."

Lanza, warmly relieved: "Well now, little lady, that's a real friendly thing you've done here. But I can't imagine—I don't get it—who in the world would want to snoop on *my* place? I mean I don't understand it. Industrial espionage, I guess. Eh?"

Toni: "That's probably it. My company specializes in *protecting* men in your position, Mr. Lanza. When I found out we'd been had . . . well, I was scared to death to tell you. But I was even more afraid *not* to tell you. Gosh, I—"

Lanza, cutting in: "Oh, say, I mean—you did right, the right thing. I admire you for that. I mean, not everyone can admit they been wrong. Uh, what'd you say this man's name was? This man that hired you?"

Toni, getting stronger: "He said his name was Kirk. The credentials looked perfect, but I'm positive now that's an alias. I could give you a description, though, if that would help."

Lanza, still hot: "Oh, sure, sure—you bet. Just

a minute, uh . . ." Chair creaking, a rustling of paper, then: "Okay, what'd this guy look like?"

Toni, thoughtful, picking words carefully: "Well, he was about medium height, I'd say. But . . . well . . . something odd about that. Uh . . . yes, odd. You know—have you ever seen a man who wears elevator shoes? I believe, yes—he wore elevator shoes, very fancy ones. Uh . . . well built, very beautifully dressed—stylish, you know. Handsome, too, a very handsome man—very white teeth, black hair, sort of dark skinned—uh . . ."

Lanza, dissatisfied with that: "Anything, uh, really distinguishing? You know—marks, scars, tattoos—anything like that?"

Toni, thinking that over: "No . . . but . . . he *reminded* me of somebody, uh . . ."

Lanza, thoughtfully: "You mean like someone on TV or the movies or something."

Toni, still working at the image: "Yes, uh . . . a singer, a *singer*, yes—uh, the man who comes from Italy, the romantic uh . . . uh . . ."

She had him hooked now; Bolan was thinking. He'd set the hook for himself.

Sure enough—Lanza, groaning: "You don't mean Enzo Stuarti!"

Toni, crowing: "That's the one! Do you know—does that mean something to you?"

Lanza, very subdued now and thoughtful: "Aw, no, no—but at least it's something to go on. Say, uh, you know how much I appreciate all this, Mrs. Davidson. You, uh, you say your fellows disappeared before they ever got this thing going? You, uh, you sure of that?"

Toni, positively: "We never turnkeyed the job,

Mr. Lanza. I believe my partners must have found out it was illegal and went to see this bogus Mr. Kirk. I'm sure they wouldn't give him details of the installation or any of the receiving gear if they even suspected—"

Lanza, relieved: "Okay, I understand. I don't want you to be worrying that pretty head about your partners. I have my ways around this town, and I want to assure you that I'll do everything I can to find those men of yours. You put your address and phone number on this pad here. I'll be getting in touch. And don't you worry. But now I'll have to ask you to excuse me. I have a million things to do and—"

Toni: "Oh, certainly. You're being very nice about this. I hope there's some way I can make it up to you. I mean . . ."

Lanza, still very subdued: "You already did, believe me. But if you don't think so, then I bet we could figure out something, couldn't we. Maybe you could take me out to dinner or something—after Mardi Gras, eh?"

Toni: "You're on. Well, you're just a marvelous man. Do you know—can you believe it?—I was scared to death to come back here!"

Lanza, laughing: "Shows how wrong you can be, huh. Listen, you really do owe me a dinner. I'm going to collect it. Soon as I turn up those partners for you, I'm going to collect."

Toni, walking away from pickup: "You know how much I appreciate . . ."

Bolan lost her there. He could hear heavy footsteps, muffled voices, the door opening. Apparently Lanza was accompanying her out.

Bolan returned quickly to the console and activated the autoswitchers, scanning and tracking her through the house and outside. When he returned forward to the optic tracking, Toni was being escorted to the gate by the same guy who'd brought her in; Lanza was nowhere in view.

As Toni's car hit the main drive, an audio scanner brought in Lanza's shouting commands, heavy with profanity and a rage that was building on itself. "Call Zeno! Tell 'im we're coming back out and goddammit we got some hot shit to discuss with the old man! If that fuckin' Carlotti is around there, he's to *stay* until we get there! Bastard, son of a bitch, what a great fuckin' ride this has been—holding the whole goddam thing together with my bare hands and these rotten fucks, *bugging* me—can you imagine?— I can't, I just can't imagine . . ."

Bolan grinned, killed the instrumentation, and poised the warwagon for another run along the backtrack.

Things were getting hot in the old town, and not just for Mardi Gras!

10: TRACKING EAST

The excited but restrained tones of Bolan's best friend in the world came clipping through the long-distance hookup between Louisiana and Massachusetts. "Well, Jesus, it's about time. I had just given you up for the third schedule in a row. Hey—you know how far it is from my joint to this damn phone booth?"

Bolan was wheeling casually along Robert E. Lee Boulevard, running in thin traffic while maintaining optic contact with the procession of Lanza vehicles several blocks ahead. "Sorry, Sticker. I've been busy."

"Sticker" was the open-line code name for Leo Turrin, an important underboss in a Massachusetts family—also an undercover federal agent. The double life of Leo Turrin tripled onto the thin edge of a knifeblade in his friendship with Mack Bolan, a fugitive from both sides of Turrin's world. They had been friends since Bolan's first campaign, in the hometown of Pittsfield.

"Yeah, I know how busy you've been," Turrin replied. "Your busy has been coming in from both sides of the street. I was on the horn with Washington 'bout an hour ago. Somebody's lighting a fire to get the federal taskforce down to New Orleans. Hal [Brognola, U.S. Department of Justice] thinks the pressure's coming via Florida—the man there, you know."

Brognola was another long-time Bolan friend and sometime ally, though chief of the "get Mack Bolan" taskforce. The divided loyalties made things very tough on a man like Hal Brognola.

Bolan told Turrin, "I'm on mobile phone, so watch it."

"Gotcha. Well, I've got that info you were pawing the ground for last night. You ready to read?"

Far ahead, the Lanza procession swerved south onto Pontchartrain Boulevard. Bolan briefly consulted a miniature light-table mounted below the dash, hit the roll-frame button to sector in the street map of that neighborhood, then grunted with satisfaction and made his turn south at Mt. Carmel Academy. He was running a parallel course, now, and maintaining track.

"You there?"

Bolan replied, "Ready to read. Go."

"Okay. It's a Saint Looey contingent, all right. Number it fifty strong and budgeted for local pickups—budget unlimited. They are now in the territory—have been for a couple of days—but staying low. If you're interested, you'd have to take about an eighty-mile drive toward Biloxi. Stop at the Edgewater Beach and look around. Unusual scenery there the past few days."

"That's local headquarters, eh?"

"That's the one. Swank joint, no connection, just the watering hole and staging area for the present campaign."

"Who's in charge of the delegation?"

Bolan swung west onto Fillmore Avenue, angling for the close-track down Pontchartrain.

Turrin was replying, "Guy name Ciglia—spell it with a C and give it an exclamation point."

"That hard, eh?"

"Yeah, that hard. He's looking for more than shortbread. If he can pull this, he's got himself a territory—that's the prize."

"Knighthood, eh?"

"That's it. So watch him. He'll be playing for keeps."

"Aren't we all?" Bolan commented, and pulled onto Pontchartrain, a block behind his party.

Turrin chuckled as he replied, "Well, that's life on the knife. And that's all I have. How's your heart?"

"Still pumping," Bolan said lightly. "How's the other side of the street look?"

"Like I said, the fires are lighting for a move against this blitzing dude in blacksuit. Hal is still in command of the situation, but he doesn't know for how much longer. He's opposed to the trip. Considers it a very bad time for manhunting in Nola. But our Florida friend has a lot of clout in some high offices, you know that. He's also about the only friend your old man there knows these days. Hal wants to just keep hands off and let the fur fall where it will. But, you know how it goes."

83

Bolan said, "Yeah. Was I hunching on target with the New York group?"

"Right on. They're backing Saint Looey right down the track. Seem to think it's now or never."

"Well, I can't let it be now," Bolan said. "And you can tell Hal I said that."

"Hell, I agree. So does Hal. He's contending that the sudden infusion of federal marshals into the situation will simply confuse things further. Secretly, chum, he's tickled to death you're there. Sees you as a balancing factor. The drift I get, though he's not flat out saying so—I get a massive move on old man Vee within the next few months. They're going to ship him out, for good and all. Then they believe they can dismantle his organization piece by piece. But not with new national leadership moving into the situation. That would set the program back years."

"Try light-years," Bolan commented.

"Yeah. Well. Do you need anything else?"

"I don't know. I have a real problem here, Sticker. Able Team."

"Huh?"

"The final two. They're on the scene and mixed in. Presently missing in action."

"Aw, shit!"

"Yeah, well—I've got to walk softly for a while. It's hurting the timing, but I've got to play the ear a bit. I'd hoped to have this scene clean before the streets go full crazy tomorrow. But now I don't know."

"Well you've got to consider the Edgewater Beach bunch. I don't see how you can do much more than jump when they jump."

"That's the problem," Bolan agreed.

"Can I help with Able Team?"

"No. So far, I think, their cover's intact. Can't risk that."

"You live a very complicated life, my friend," Turrin said.

"Look who's sounding off," Bolan replied. "Listen —tell Hal to contact Petro in New Orleans. I passed the guy a bundle today. Hal will find it interesting."

"Who the hell is Petro?"

"Hal will know. Just tell him, huh?"

"Sure. You sound tired."

"Name of the game."

Turrin sighed into the connection. "Watch that reserve strength. You're heading into a lot of crazies. Nobody's going to quit easy this time."

"That's the worry, but it's also the hope."

"Whatever that means."

"It means," Bolan explained, "that I'm counting on them knocking out one another."

"You can't count on that too strongly. From where I sit, all the odds are on the top in this North-South game."

"I do need something, Sticker."

"Run it, I'll try."

"The local pretty boy here . . . you know who?"

"Shoes from Rome?—yeah."

"Where do you read him?"

"Top of the list," Turrin said immediately. "Heir apparent, second to none. Why?"

"He's playing games for somebody, maybe for himself but it sounds nutty that way."

"Insurance games?"

"Could be. Or it could be he's trying to work

both sides of the street. Uh, this is where Able Team entered. You know their specialty. Pretty Boy contracted them to specialize on Money Man."

"No shit!"

"None at all. As of just last week. It could be under orders from Mr. Vee, of course. I'd sure like to know the name of his game. Think you could come up with any sort of feel?"

"How much time do I have?"

"No time at all."

"Okay. I'll try to meet that schedule. When will you beep?"

Bolan checked the time and replied, "Let's say two hours."

Turrin chuckled. "Yeah, that's what you said—no time at all. I'll try, buddy. But no promises."

"Thanks, friend. Watch your swinger."

Turrin's dry laugh was still rattling the connection when Bolan switched off and began pulling abreast of the Lanza convoy. He was counting noses and probable firepower as he made the run-by, and a side-mounted camera was recording the event for later close evaluation.

It was a full head party.

Rocco Lanza was gunning for bear—and the fur would soon be flying all around that town.

Bolan grinned soberly and surged on ahead, abandoning the track at the I-10 cloverleaf and running east while the six-car head party continued southward.

It was a rather safe bet that Lanza was indeed headed for "the Farm" for a confrontation over the bugging incident. He may or may not find Carlotti there; Bolan was betting on the *not*.

Toni had not been tailed from the lakefront. There was no need to worry about her for the moment.

The worry was for Able Group—and Bolan's immediate instincts had drawn a likely scenario from the fact that Carlotti was the employer. The scenario ran along a typical Mafia pattern. Anyone brought in from the outside to perform a delicate Mafia mission seldom survived to profit from the assignment. The payoff was usually a bullet in the head and a cement coffin. Bolan held very feeble hopes for the fate of Blancanales and Schwarz. The only ray of hope—and it was a dim one—was the knowledge that the surveillance routine on the Lanza joint had never been worked. It seemed unlikely that Carlotti would terminate his contractors before taking delivery of the job. There could have been other complications, of course—but Bolan had to run with that one hope, and he was doing so.

Play it by ear and walk softly—this was his understanding of the only role available to him for the moment. In such a role, there was little to be gained in New Orleans for at least the next few hours. Events that were now beyond his manipulation would have to set the pace for a while.

Except for one consideration.

And Mack Bolan was now en route to Mississippi. The time had come to scout—and maybe roust—the Northern army.

11: STAGING AREA

Bolan's memories of the Mississippi Gulf Coast recalled a 28-mile strand of white sand beach—broken only at the center by the port of Gulfport—a palm-lined drive along U.S. 90 from St. Louis Bay to the Bay of Biloxi, the four-lane divided highway separating the white sand from the stately old mansions lining that drive—here and there a motel or a restaurant, now and then a private pier extending into the placid waters of the sound, offshore islands appearing faintly on the horizon. Beyond Gulfport would be found the more glittery aspects of life at the water's edge—luxury motels back to back, nightclubs and fashionable restaurants, flashy marinas and amusement parks, culminating finally in the frenzy of Biloxi with her hundred and one bars and dives, strip joints and hamburger stands, clip-joint casinos and fleshstands, and all the trappings that earned the subtitle of "Little Las Vegas."

That was the tourist's-eye view. There was more.

For instance, the amalgam of local cultures that echoed and mingled the early and shifting influences of Spain, France, England, and Africa. A quarter of a mile inland from those man-made beaches could be found sweet-smelling jungles, Cajun communities, rural ghettos, wealthy plantations. Gulfport was a bustling and thriving seaport and commercial center, Biloxi the home of a large and stable fishing fleet. A few miles from St. Louis Bay was a large NASA test site; professionals from that facility had made homes in Bay St. Louis, Pass Christian, Long Beach—and a few as far away as Gulfport. Many of the beachfront homes were owned by natives of New Orleans, Jackson, and other nearby inland cities. Biloxi had an air force base and training center. Pascagoula, just across Biloxi Bay, was an active shipbuilding center.

The flavor of the area was thus a mixed one. Add to that the universal flavoring of a seacoast resort, and it would seem virtually impossible to pinpoint an alien presence along the 28-mile stretch of sun and fun. Mack Bolan, however, possessed a special nose for the aliens he sought; if they were here, he would find them.

There'd been some changes in the Edgewater Beach area since Bolan's last visit quite a few years back. A large, beautiful shopping mall had been added to the local scenery. A new marina, impressively modern, was connected to the luxury hotel by a pedestrian bridge over the highway. Other changes—some good and some not so good—were noted as he made a slow pass along the eastward leg of U.S. 90, then circled back to enter the sprawling grounds of the landmark hotel.

The time was just past noon, the sun high in the sky and warming to the landscape. Bolan donned dark glasses, yachting cap, casual jacket over the Beretta shoulder rig, left the warwagon parked conspicuously between a sports car and a limousine, and headed directly for the lobby.

Guys in small groups were strolling aimlessly about the golfgreen-type lawn. Some stood about idly in the shade of the porch. Still others prowled restlessly about the lobby area. Young guys, most of them in their twenties or maybe early thirties—well dressed, obviously intelligent—entirely innocuous to the casual observer.

Bolan knew better.

They were triggermen—killing time until the designated time and place to begin killing men.

The new breed, the sophisticates—fairly well educated, reasonably well read, articulate—they could join most any group of bored businessmen or traveling salesmen and pass themselves off as the same.

And the placard just inside the lobby told the story of this particular "convention":

MIDWESTERN TRADE GROUP
CONFERENCE ROOM D

Bolan bypassed that invitation and went instead to a house phone near the desk. "Mr. Ciglia's room, please," he told the operator.

"That is spelled . . . ?"

"With a C. He's here with the trade group."

"No, sir, I'm sorry. We don't have a Ciglia."

Not by that name, anyway, Bolan thought. He told the honey-Southern voice at the other end of the house phone, "I guess he hasn't registered yet."

"Maybe you misunderstood the name," she suggested helpfully. "We show Mr. William P. Stigni as the chairman of Midwestern."

Bolan chuckled, with a mental nod to Southern hospitality, and replied, "Oh, yes, sure. From St. Louis—right?"

"Yes, sir. Mr. Stigni left word that he will be in Conference Room D for the afternoon. Want me to ring?"

"Thanks, no. I'll find him." Bolan hung up, lit a cigarette, gave the lobby area a final casing, then wandered around until he found the conference room.

The door stood ajar. Three men were in there. One sat at a long table, playing solitaire. The other two stood at a large map tacked to the back wall, playing with stickpins and conversing in monosyllables.

The guy at the table looked up from his cards as Bolan entered. "Yes?" he asked coolly. It was a challenge, not a greeting.

Using the same tone of voice, Bolan replied, "Mr. Stigni."

A guy of about thirty stepped away from the map to give the visitor a quick once-over. Heavyset, dark eyes with smile wrinkles, but a nasty-looking mouth. The eyes lingered on the yachting cap as he said, "I'm Stigni. What do you want?"

Bolan told him, "Wrong guy. I knew a guy named Stigni. In Texas. You're not him."

"Larry?" the heavy one asked, interested.

"That's the one. They called him Larry Awful."

"I'm Bill. Larry was my cousin."

"Was?"

"He's dead."

Bolan leaned against the wall, took a hard pull at his cigarette, toyed with the sunglasses, then said, "I'm sorry."

The guy shrugged. "Comes to us all sooner or later. It came to Larry sooner. You, uh, you were associated with my cousin?"

"Briefly," Bolan replied, not exactly lying. He'd executed Larry Stigni in Dallas during the Texas campaign. "I did a bit of work with Joe Quaso once."

"Joe's dead, too," Stigni reported soberly.

"Yeah, I heard about him."

"You, uh, looking for a connection here?"

Bolan dropped into a chair near the door, relaxed, legs stretched forward. "Not exactly." He tugged at the yachting cap. "Getting a bit of rest, between jobs. My New York office contacted me this morning. Said maybe I should look in on a guy named Ciglia. Said maybe he could use some technical advice in, uh, in my specialty."

The other guy at the map had swiveled about to give Bolan an interested inspection. The one at the table decked his cards, pushed them away, and moved his chair clear of the table. His jacket gaped, revealing hardware beneath.

Bolan showed him a sober smile and said, "Relax."

The guy at the map laughed softly.

Stigni asked Bolan, "What'd you say your name was?"

"I didn't say. You can call me Frankie. Where's Ciglia?"

Stigni said, "He's out on the—"

92

The other guy stopped him with a bark. "Bill!"

Bolan chuckled, slowly got to his feet, went to the table, shuffled through the deck of cards until he found the right one, turned the ace of spades face up atop the deck, returned to his chair and sat down. "Where's Ciglia?" he asked again.

Stigni shot a reproachful glance toward the guy at the map. "Jerry's getting in a few holes of golf," he told the man of the black ace.

This was better, Bolan was thinking. The black ace was a symbol for the lord high executioner of the Mafia world—an office operated directly from *La Commissione*—a sort of identity card for their agents. In the strange protocol of the world of Mafia, it was bad form to exhibit any sort of curiosity toward that office or toward the men serving it. It was far worse than bad form to show any disrespect or open hostility.

The guy at the wall, a smooth-faced deadeye with "torpedo" stamped all over him, had undergone a total transformation. "How long you in town for, Frankie?" he asked amiably.

"Just passing through," Bolan told him, just as amiably. He winked and added, "On my way to Mardi Gras."

This produced a round of laughter. Stigni brought on another chorus of cackles with the declaration, "We thought we might look in on that, ourselves." Then he told Bolan, "I'll send someone out to get Jerry. He only left about half an hour ago, probably won't be back 'til—"

Bolan waved away the offer and said, "Aw, don't bother him. I just dropped by to say 'ay'—maybe look up some old friends. How're things in Saint Loo?"

"Getting tough," Stigni replied.

"Whole damned town's crumbling to hell," said smooth-face. "Whole damned state, I guess."

"It's that kid governor," the kid triggerman groused.

Stigni sighed, adding, "Crime commissions in KC and pimp wars in Rolla."

"Well," Bolan commented consolingly, "things'll look better after Mardi Gras. Eh?"

"Yeah," all agreed, laughing.

Bolan said, "Guess you got it nailed down pretty well, eh?"

"We think so," Stigni said, then immediately changed his mind about that. "Or we *did*. One or two loose ends right now." He made a vague wave toward the map. "Got some inside poop, you know, got everything spotted and all. We figured it to go zip-zip, like that, quiet as snow falling. Nobody'd know 'til it was too late to know. But now Jerry's not so sure. I guess you heard about this Bolan freak banging around over there. It's probably going to take a war, now."

This "Bolan freak" had gone to the map for a look. It was of New Orleans and suburbs. Stickpin pennants in X'd circles marked the spots for assassination, with no surprises for Bolan.

"How's the recruiting going?" he asked casually.

"Pretty good," Stigni reported happily. "Picked up thirty through this morning. Expect to have another thirty or forty on board by tonight."

"That'll give you—what?—about 100 to 125 guns?"

"Yeah."

"Good boys?"

"Good enough."

The guy at the table chuckled and added, "Good enough to front-line. But you don't exactly get command class off of *these* streets."

"We got a few over from the Mobile-Pensacola area," smooth-face argued.

"Same damn streets," the other replied, snickering.

"Frankie" was taking his departure. He said, "Well—tell Ciglia I'm on my way in to look at this Bolan problem. Maybe I can save it some over there."

"Hey, that's great!" Stigni crowed. "Stick a Union Jack up that bastard's ass for me, huh, Frankie?"

"Jerry's going to be pissed off we didn't send for him," smooth-face decided. "He'd sure like to meet you, I know."

"Tell him we'll meet for Mardi Gras."

The guy smiled broadly. "Sure, okay. I'll tell him, Frankie."

Bolan waved airily and walked out of there.

There was no need for smooth-face to tell Jerry anything.

The Executioner was headed for the pro shop. He'd deliver the message for himself . . . in his own way.

12: UPSTAGED

The pro shop was deserted. Bolan reached past a "gone to lunch" sign on the counter and pulled the book around to see what it could reveal.

Apparently most of the Edgewater golfers preferred the early morning hours. No parties had been booked since 10:00, except for a threesome that went out at 11:45 under the name "Jackson Co."

Bolan studied the layout of the course and ran a timeline on the latest threesome, then returned to the warwagon and headed inland along a narrow road that paralleled the golf course for a distance, pulling off finally onto a cross-country approach.

He found the spot he had hoped to find and set up shop in a stand of pines overlooking the tee for the eighth hole.

The range would be about 500 yards. He broke out the optics and refined that figure to 480 on the nose—par one, straight down the fairway.

He selected the Weatherby Mark IV for the task, a

heavy-frame piece, built up even heavier, that would drop a charging grizzly from a thousand yards out.

Pointblank range for the Weatherby was 400 yards —that is, the range at which trajectory rise and drop equalled and cancelled. He consulted the graphs and nicked the sniperscope to the proper correction, then took a wind reading and decided there would be no wind factor.

He scanned and sectored the tee area with the telescopic sights while running a mental choreography of the probable movements down there—considering backgrounds, foregrounds, possible interventions across the target track, target approach, target escape, target zero.

And then he waited.

He filled the wait with thoughts of the chummy little *tête à tête* with Stigni and the other cheerful cannibals—and he thought of Vannaducci, Carlotti, Lanza, and all those of the decaying New Orleans "family." He thought of Ciglia and his dreams of empire, and he thought of the St. Louis mob and the New York coalition—and, yeah, Mack Bolan knew his enemies.

They were not "families"—certainly not a brotherhood of "friends."

Bolan was not the worst enemy the Mafia had. Nor were the feds or the crime commissions nor all the cops combined everywhere.

The Mafia's worst enemy was itself.

Until Bolan came along, their greatest fear had been of one another.

Family *hell!*

A pack of wild dogs was more like it. Dogs that ran together and brought down the prey together, then frequently attacked one another over the disposition of the spoils. Cannibals, competing for the fruits of the hunt, each determined to the death to hog the greatest share or come out on top of the choicest territory—cannibals who laughed together and joked it up over organized betrayal, systematic deceit, mass assassination of their own kind.

Yes, Mack Bolan knew his enemies.

As a group they represented the basest aspects of the human species. They were evolutionary throwbacks, these guys, forging a Stone Age philosophy in a never-let-die jungle of survival.

He felt no quiver of conscience whatever for returning guys like these to the age in which they belonged.

Somebody had to stop these guys.

Sure, Bolan had heard all the arguments against his own approach to the problem. But the other approaches had never worked. The official agencies had been "addressing" the Mafia problem in this country since long before the Chicago crusades of Ness and his feds, way back before Bolan's birth. Forty years and more of "addressing" had gone by —and the problem had just gotten larger and more unmanageable. These Stone-agers owned courts, and legislatures, and governors' mansions. They had handles on the Congress, and now the question was being raised as to whether they had access to the White House even.

A motley collection of Stone Age hoods were being called "the invisible second government of the nation." Bolan knew that it was no exaggeration. He knew also about the "little Wall Street" that was bleeding the national economy, and he knew that soon the Stone-Agers from around the world would have earned the right to be called "the second invisible financial establishment of the planet Earth."

The Stone Age was overcoming the twentieth century.

That was the reality that haunted and motivated Mack Bolan. What the hell was personal conscience in the face of all that?

Bolan would do what he knew had to be done. If, after all, it was wrong—then at least he would have a lot of company in hell.

Then the wait was over. All the thoughts and second thoughts swirled and blended into the focal field of a twenty-power sniperscope as a motorized golf buggy swung into the crosshairs, just off the tee for the eighth hole—and Bolan knew that this was, finally, what he was all about; it narrowed down to this: there stood the enemy in his crosshairs and yes, the Executioner had a twentieth-century solution to the problems of the Stone Age.

He lifted off the scope and went to binoculars for an area sweep, ensuring that no stray bystanders were in the target zone, then he studied the target area itself for visual confirmation of the identification his hackles had already made.

Two of them were guntoters and nothing else, not even making a pretense of golfing. They stood to either side of the tee to keep up a constant, nervous surveillance of the surrounding areas—young, mean-looking guys who'd probably murder their own mothers if the boss suggested that they do so.

The third man wore slacks and a bright polo shirt, also a cap with a smoked plastic visor. He looked about thirty-five, darkly handsome, a bit chunky with plenty of hard muscle beneath the layer of flab. Sweat soaked through the knit shirt and glistened on hairy arms, though it was not a particularly warm day.

And there was no question of identity, though Bolan had never seen that face before. This was Ciglia, the little general from the North—camped out and golfing a few miles from Jeff Davis's *Beauvoir*.

Bolan returned to the scope and watched through twenty powers of magnification as the guy washed a ball then paced around the tee getting his sightings and wondering, probably, which wood he should use for this drive.

A serious golfer. Yeah. This guy would do everything seriously.

The scope swung on to etch the spots where the bodyguards stood and to once more run through the choreography of reaction.

The task would require three rounds at rapid fire, X to Y to Z without once lifting off the scope to search for reacting secondary targets.

The primary target was not a man. It was a small, white sphere with a blue dot stamped into its rubber hide, and it was at that moment being placed upon the tee, scrubbed and shiny for its debut and demise.

Bolan's angle of vision for the 480-yard shot was right down the fairway off the tee, behind the swing. As Ciglia's club swung back and reached its highest point, the hammer of the Weatherby fell onto the chambered round. Four thousand pounds of muzzle energy beat that swing and propelled a sizzling 300-grain chunk of hot iron that screamed in just ahead of the descending wood.

The small white globe dissolved on the tee, too late for Ciglia to check the swing. He went on through and lost his balance in the reaction, falling forward across the secondary target track, that shocked face looming momentarily in the restricted field of vision as the scope swung along the Y-plot.

Y-target was no more than a startled face frozen in the direction of thunder; again the hammer closed a fraction of an inch gap to reach out a quarter mile and explode into that face, and already Big Thunder was tracking the Z-course of panicky reaction.

An ear with curly black hair framing it flashed through that track—a descending one, moving hastily from full vertical to stretched horizontal as the target flung himself groundward in a spinning dive —and the reticles were waiting for him there at the end of the track. Bolan's curled finger traveled a distance of perhaps two millimeters and Z-target promptly ceased to exist.

That third big boom was still rattling the air down there at the eighth tee as the Executioner switched to binoculars for target evaluation.

The two bodyguards would not be with the boss in New Orleans. Goodly portions of their skulls would never leave the soil of Mississippi.

The boss himself was still scrambling for cover, head down and ass high and no longer pondering the inexplicable behavior of a golf ball that exploded on the downswing. The serious golfer was now a very serious survival candidate in the oldest

101

game of all, sprinting for the good life and the protection of the little mound of the seventh hole.

Bolan shouldered the Weatherby and withdrew to the warwagon.

He had not wanted the general of the Northern army dead in Mississippi. He wanted him alive in New Orleans. Alive but just a little less cocky, a lot more cautious, and mad as hell.

Ciglia had his message from "Frankie."

No doubt a call would be going into New York within the next few minutes. Certain embarrassing questions would have to be asked, and even more embarrassing conclusions drawn when those questions were answered.

Yeah. The Northern army had their damned message from New Orleans.

Now let them think about it.

13: READINGS

Bolan was monitoring the state police radio net and knew when the official reaction had set in from the Edgewater Beach strike. If he was reading their signals correctly, they were going balls out in an attempt to seal off the entire beach area. The swiftness of the reaction came as a bit of a surprise. The state force must have already been on some sort of standby alert, and now they were moving very quickly to bottle him in.

Most of the official attention was moving toward the bridge at Biloxi for eastbound traffic, toward the interstate route out of Gulfport for northbound and westbound traffic. Bolan had already decided to shun Interstate 10 for the return to New Orleans, continuing instead along the coastal U.S. 90 route, at least to the Louisiana line.

As he was cruising past Pass Christian he intercepted the signal dispatching a single car from the Bay St. Louis-Waveland beat to the west end of the

Bay St. Louis bridge—and Bolan lost that race by about six carlengths.

It was a worry, sure; the last thing the Executioner needed at this stage of the game, or at any stage, was a police checkout of his new wheels. But it was not a panic situation.

The official "artist's sketch" of his face was not that close. He had the best credentials money could buy. The gear in the warwagon was well camouflaged and would pass anything but the most determined scrutiny.

Cops on roadblock duty did not usually tear a vehicle down to its wheels—not unless something really aroused their suspicions. They would be looking for "probable cause" for a real shakedown—and Bolan did not normally give them that much.

And for this one there was but one car, one trooper. Bolan shook his head over that. It was suicide duty, given the wrong kind of fugitive.

He inched along to the inspection point, then lowered his window and showed the guy an understanding grin. "Somebody steal a seagull or something?" he joked.

It was a young cop, well schooled in police procedure as well as good manners to visiting tourists. He smiled soberly and told the Executioner, "A shooting down the coast, sir. Routine check. Your driver's license and vehicle registration, please."

Bolan handed them over.

"Any other identification, sir?"

Bolan handed him a press card, two credit cards, and was digging for more as he casually chatted, "Didn't this use to be a toll bridge? Last time I was through here . . ."

104

"Not since Camille, sir."

"Since what?"

"Hurricane Camille. It destroyed the station, and I guess the state figured that was as good a time as any to close it for good."

"Hey, those hurricanes are hell. Did you say a shooting?"

"Yes, sir." The trooper waved away further identification and passed the cards back. "Sorry for the delay, sir. You may proceed."

Bolan touched the bill of his cap and proceeded.

A city car came tearing up to reinforce the state's finest just as the warwagon pulled away from the lineup. Bolan relaxed and began breathing "off the numbers" as he rolled slowly through the outskirts of the small community of Bay St. Louis.

It was no reflection on the trooper that Bolan breezed past so easily. Far more experienced men than he had gazed straight at the Executioner without seeing him—many times, in many places. Besides which, the vehicle itself would hardly raise the eyes of those searching for a fleeing fugitive.

There would be no more roadblocks across this route. There was time now to think of other things, and Bolan had plenty to think about.

New Orleans was about an hour away. With luck, he could make it to the corner of Claiborne and Canal by two o'clock for a rendezvous with Toni Blancanales. Meanwhile, he was an hour late for the intelligence contact with Leo Turrin. And he was probably not within range of a mobile operator. He tried anyway, surprisingly raised one on good signal conditions, and placed his call to the New England number.

Leo's guarded voice responded to the first ring. "Yeah?"

"Sorry I'm late."

"I'm getting used to it. But what the hell're you trying to do?"

"Stay alive. Why?"

"I was worried. Just finished a call to the contract desk in New York, fishing for words on you. The whole damn place is in turmoil. What'd you do down there?"

Bolan chuckled. "A light roust," he reported.

"Light, hell. It got all the chickens off the roost. They're sending a top squad down to the beach by special jet."

"Great," Bolan commented. "That'll make our man even more upset."

"The headshed is flapping about information leaks right now. They're wondering how you glommed onto the beach digs so quick."

"You covered?"

"Oh, sure. I always use the back door. Pays to have chatty friends. Hey—it looks like you're right about Shoes from Rome. He's been seen skulking around *Commissione* headquarters several times during the past few months. And somebody else."

"Who's that?"

"The wearer of the twisted cross."

That meant *gestapo*, which translated to *enforcer* —who, in New Orleans, could only be Enrico Campenaro, Vannaducci's strong right arm.

Bolan said, "That's very interesting. How does it read to you?"

"Same way it does to you," Turrin replied. "They've turned on the old man, figuring it's sweeter to eat him than to run the risk of getting buried with him."

Bolan growled, "Yeah."

After all this time and bloodshed, treachery such as this still rumbled at his guts. From all reports, Marco Vannaducci loved Tommy Carlotti like an only son—which the old man had never had—and which, now, he could not even adopt. As for Campenaro, he'd been nothing but a Bourbon Street button commando when the old man took him in, bathed him and put decent clothes on him, and handed him an empire to guard.

Yes. A rotten place, this world of Mafia.

"You still there?" Turrin was wondering.

"Yeah. Sorry, Sticker. I was just thinking about what a rotten world you and I dirty ourselves with."

"Name of our game, buddy," the old friend reminded him.

"You talk to Hal yet?" Bolan glumly wondered.

"I did. He sent his thanks. Then he talked to your man there, called me back, and sent thanks again. He says there's no way he can make Nola until after Mardi Gras." Turrin chuckled. "He's about to get kicked upstairs."

"To what, and when?" Bolan inquired, very interested.

"Somebody evidently doesn't like the way he's running OrgCrime. It looks like he's going to be an assistant attorney general, in another division, and damned soon."

Bolan said, "Well, well."

"Something is very rotten in Washington, Striker."

"Yeah," Bolan growled.

"You're thinking!" Turrin declared accusingly.

"You bet I am."

"Keep your ass clear of Washington! Last time you damned near—"

Bolan cut in with, "Hey, hey, I have to get out of Nola, first. You have any more gems for me?"

"I guess not. I very delicately tried a ripple about your Able friends and struck out. Nothing. If someone up here is in on that type of operation, then they're keeping it very close."

Bolan said, "Okay. If you were standing here I'd kiss you. I—"

"Don't try, just don't try," the man from Mass growled.

Bolan laughed and signed off.

Then a dark mood settled over him and he kicked the warwagon into a hot run toward New Orleans.

The whole country was in a mess. With cancer of the brain, what hope could there be for the body?

Yes, Sticker—the Striker was thinking.

He was thinking about embattled good men, like Hal Brognola, trying desperately to hack their way through the entangled jungle growth that had become official Washington—about Stone Age politics and a crumbling national faith in institutions of government—and with what cause . . . with what *cause!*

And, yes, there were other fronts to probe . . . as soon as possible. The New Orleans wrap-up would have to come quickly and decisively. He'd set them up for the knockout—then pulled his punch in concern for a couple of old friends who were probably dead anyway.

It was a lousy way to push a war.

Toni had said the right words. Pol himself would

have roared, "On with the game, the game's gotta go on!"

"Yeah," Bolan growled aloud to himself.

The game was damned sure going to go on.

14: WALLS

Lieutenant Petro rubbed aching eyes and told the confining walls of his office, "I just don't believe that guy."

He did, of course. There was no way to cut the guy short. But Jack Petro had never come up against any individual who could just keep on going through night and day without stopping occasionally for a breather or a few winks of sleep or—for God's sake —a drink of water or something.

For that reason he had at first been disinclined to credit Bolan with the Mississippi strike. How, he reasoned, could a guy raise all the hell that guy had raised in this town during the night and early morning and then truck it on over to the Gulf Coast and pull something like that for lunch?

Then the details had come in from Gulfport. Head hits, from about five hundred yards out, two of them in rapid fire—across a distance of five damned football fields? Against armed, cagey professionals who must have been halfway expecting something like that in the first place?

Then the clincher.

The nervy shit had shot a *golf ball* off a *tee* to open the formalities!

So, sure. It *had* to be Bolan. And what a goddam guy!

The gold-braided fed Brognola had made no secret of his feelings for the guy. Loved him like a brother! Tried to get him to accept fed sponsorship, several times. The guy *refused!* Imagine that! Refusing total amnesty, complete with secret badge and license to hunt. That told something about the guy. But, what? Maybe the guy had an overpowering death instinct—*wanted* to die young.

"*Bullshit!*" Petro yelled at the wall.

The guy wasn't *dying!* He was the livingest son of a bitch Jack Petro had ever heard of!

So maybe that was the answer. Yeah, maybe it was.

The rackets cop debated with his fatigue for a moment then picked up the phone and called his counterpart at State.

"What're they doing in Mississippi?" he asked the other wallbanger.

"Mostly running around holding their heads in their hands," was the wry response. "Same thing we're doing here."

"That figures," Petro growled. "I mean what're they doing about their nonesteemed visitors from upcountry?"

"It's kind of interesting that you should ask that," State replied.

111

"How about giving me an interesting answer," Petro suggested.

"Well—they haven't broken any laws, you know. Not that anyone knows about. Even the dead men were carrying gun permits."

"Local endorsement?"

"You bet. And here's a kicker. They're Louisiana-endorsed also."

Petro whistled. "Who gave it to them?"

"We're checking that."

"Yeah, sure." The NOPD rackets specialist threw a pencil at the wall. "That'll end at the fucking wall, just like everything else."

"Don't take it so personally," State advised. "One of these days we'll get all the walls down around here."

"Fat chance," Petro groused.

"Then the view will be so blinding, we'll probably start building new ones."

It was a cynical profession these men belonged to.

Petro sent that thought crashing into the wall of his office as he told his friend at State, "I'd like to be kept advised on the movements of that bunch from St. Louis."

"We're in constant liaison with Mississippi," he was assured. "They're still trying to come to a decision about their presence over there."

"What's our official position on the matter?"

"Leave them be and keep them under watch. We're almost certain that their presence is tied into the Mack Bolan problem. We regard the two problems as one and the same. We don't want them

112

rousted from there just to get up and move over here."

"They're coming anyway, you know," Petro said.

"There's that feeling, sure. Our guess is that they're just using Mississippi as a base. At least we know now that they are around and—"

"Thanks to Bolan, no thanks to our own goddam—"

"—and that they've been coming in over the past three days. If Mississippi invites them out of the state, they'll just go somewhere else close by and mob up again. Hell, we're saying leave them be. And keep us advised of movements."

"Those bastards are coming to Mardi Gras!" Petro declared disgustedly.

"Well . . . maybe so, maybe not."

"I have it on eminent authority that they are!"

"Whose eminence?"

"Mack fucking Bolan, that's whose eminence!"

A brief silence, then: "Really? Old buddy of yours, or something?"

"New one," Petro growled. "He sent me a package of dynamite this morning. It's going to blow some walls down, too, if I can keep it out of the wrong hands."

"I'd like to see it."

"You will. Copies, anyway. But not until I have the originals properly sealed away under a dead man's trigger."

"My, we're getting paranoid," State declared, a bit grumpily.

"Betcher ass we are, and we're staying that way, buddy. We live longer that way." .

"Jack . . . come over. We need to get heads together. And bring that shit with you."

"Nothing doing," Petro said. "I'm sort of half expecting the guy to call again. I want to be here if he does. I think maybe he never sleeps. I'm so damned tired, I'm dizzy."

"What guy?"

"Bolan, you dummy."

"Hell, he's in Mississippi."

"Was, dummy, *was*. Very briefly, I'd bet."

"You really think he'll contact you?"

"Yeah, that's what I really think, wallbanger."

"I'll come over there, then."

"Do that. And I'll show you something to blow the walls right out of your mind."

The rackets specialist hung up the telephone with a crash. He lit a cigarette, took a deep drag, glared at the walls of the office that was hemming him in and tucking him neatly—then he got slowly to his feet and went to the nearest one, pleasantly said, "Hi, wall; fuck you, wall"—and ground the cigarette into it clear to the palm of his hand.

He knew why Bolan would not accept that amnesty license.

Walls, that's why. Walls of the mind and soul and body. A guy like Bolan would not stand for them—hell no, not any, not ever.

And that was mostly why Jack Petro admired him so.

15: THE PLOY

Bolan picked up I-10 just below Slidell and left it at the Canal offramp, swinging onto Claiborne and spotting Toni almost immediately, though he was ten minutes late for the rendezvous.

She'd changed clothes and done something different to her hair, but there was no problem recognizing her—she was some kind of gal, and Bolan was not surprised to find his heart lifting in anticipation of their meeting.

She did a slow double-take at the warwagon as it slid by, then scrambled aboard with a happy sigh when the center door opened in her face and the familiar voice called out, "Come aboard!"

Bolan pulled away immediately, with the girl swaying in the aisle. She moved forward to the cab exclaiming, "Nice! Very nice! Home is the warrior, huh?"

"Secret weapon," he said, grinning at her in the mirror. "Come on in."

She slid into the passenger seat forward, bounced on it, said, "Wow, sexy," then started bawling.

Bolan gave her silence and an understanding atmosphere as he maneuvered clear of those busy streets and back onto the interstate. As he cloverleafed south toward the Greater New Orleans Bridge, Toni got it back together, gave him an embarrassed scrutiny, and told him, "Well, that takes care of the waterworks for another week." She rubbed angrily at the reddened eyes, laughed shakily, and declared, "I pulled it off, Mack. I walked right in there and spilled my guts all over Lanza's desk—and he bought it, all of it."

"I know," he replied musingly. "Good show, Toni."

"How did you know? I've been listening to the radio. You've been over playing on the damn beaches. How could you—?"

He said, "I was with you every step of the way."

"In spirit, maybe," she argued, scoffing good-naturedly. "I'm not that dumb. I know when I'm—were you?"

"No spirits involved," Bolan said. He activated the optic reflector and swung it over for her viewing. "Use the red lever for scanning horizontally, the black for vertical. The little knob there at the bottom is for focus."

She was a great one for double-takes, pulling the routine again from Bolan's granite profile to the little viewscreen. Then she understood and bent to the task, a moment later whispering, "Right on! This is fabulous!" She swiveled in the seat, seeking the optic target with the unaided eye and locating it. "That building is a mile away!"

116

He said, "Yeah. The ears are just as good. Also have radio surveillance capability." He swung the reflector back into place and deactivated it. "I double teamed you into Lanza's joint." He gave her a quick smile. "You're some saleswoman."

"I've been told I could sell rosary beads to Baptists," she said, smiling back. "They say it's a gift. Could I sell you something, Mr. Bad?"

"Like what?"

"Like anything. You name it."

There was a suggestive opening he did not wish to pursue at the moment. Instead, he asked her, "Think you could sell a quarter of a million dollars to a punk who's never owned more than a thousand?"

She blinked rapidly at that before replying, "So what would he buy the quarter million with?"

"Maybe his life. And a safe return for a couple of Mack Bolan's old friends."

Toni cried, "Whoof! I knew it! You've got a plan!"

"A ploy, anyway," Bolan admitted. "But the game will center around you, again." He gave her a quick, oblique look as he swung off the expressway. She waited quietly as he maneuvered the outsized vehicle onto an angle for the river front. Then he added, "And much more dangerous this time."

"Hey!" she exclaimed angrily. "I told you those waterworks were my ration for the week! Don't you dare start softing me out!"

"Think you can take the heat, eh?"

"Heat you've never seen before, heat!" she huffed.

He chuckled and halted the warwagon in the shadows of a Water Street warehouse and pulled the girl into his war room, sat her down, and gave her a moment of steady, cool gaze.

117

She cooled right back at him, finally giving way to a quivering smile.

He smiled back as he asked her, "Do you have a private detective license?"

She nodded. "Sure. Can't operate without it. We observe the legalities. And we're registered here."

He said, "Okay. Carry a gun?"

She opened her purse and showed him a tiny lady's special, a nickel plated .25 Auto with pearl grips. "It's legal, too," she assured him.

"Great for starting races," he commented on the little weapon. "If you want to stop a guy with that, though, you'd better go for the mouth."

She made an unpleasant face. "Just hope I never have to. Don't worry, though—I could. Rosie saw to that. I must have fired fifty jillion rounds into moving targets. But I—in the *mouth?*—seriously?"

He nodded. "Straight through the ivories. When you play, play for keeps." He slid back a panel and produced a fat attaché case. "This is the quarter mil," he told her.

Her mind was obviously still with the previous subject, but she recovered quickly to ask, "Who do I sell it to?"

He withdrew a list from his breast pocket and gave it to her.

She scanned the list quickly, eyes widening as they raised to a flickering inspection of his face. "All of these?"

He nodded. "It's not exactly a Sunday school class, either. It's a collection of pimps, pushers, runners, streetcorner bookies, freelance hitmen—you name the illness, it's somewhere on that list. I had other plans for them. But I guess . . ."

Toni's attention had reverted to the list of names. "Are these addresses still good?"

"As of about dawn today, yes. One or two may have left town suddenly. But there's still a large field to play to. These people all work for Tommy Carlotti —your Mr. Kirk."

"What's my sales pitch?"

"Play that by your own ear. But here's the basics: Tommy Carlotti is not long for this world. Mack Bolan is very unhappy with this guy, for snatching his two friends. Carlotti is now wearing the mark of the beast. Add to that another angle for a funeral: Carlotti is crossing his *capo*, Marco Vannaducci. He's playing footsie with a New York crowd. Vannaducci knows, or he's going to know very soon. These boys are going to lose their sponsor. More than that, they're going to lose a home. War is brewing all along these streets. When the smoke settles, there will be no territories for anybody for a long, long time. So here's a chance for some smart guy to get out of it clean, before the war starts, and with a quarter mil in his jeans."

Toni's eyes were wide, speculative, as her mind elaborated on that theme. She said, "It plays. But . . . could any of these men actually *know* anything?"

"Probably not, but they are in a position to nose around and find out. It's hard to keep a secret in this crowd, especially with a bundle of money tied to it. Then of course there's always the off chance that one of these hoods is already sitting squarely on the problem."

"They could form partnerships," the girl mused. "Organize, fan out, go through the town like a—it'd be like a treasure hunt with a real treasure at the

119

end. How do I convince them of that? That they'll get the money?"

He smiled soberly and told her, "First you sweeten the pot with a thousand down to every guy you talk to. It's their weakness, a scent they can't refuse. Give him the thousand whether he expresses an interest or not. The interest will grow. And it's the best way I can think of to cause a ripple—giving money away. Pretty soon they'll be coming to *you*. This is where your hazard lies, most of it. Remember, these guys do not live by the Boy Scout oath. You've got to make it clear that Mack Bolan is your client. He's holding the money. He will deliver the money to the boys who turn over, alive and well, these two missing friends."

"Where do they turn them over? How can they be sure they'll get their money?"

"They'll get it because Bolan says they will. They know how I operate. They'll accept that. They're to make the contact when they have the goods. They'll be told where the exchange will take place."

"You're really going to give away all that money?"

Bolan shrugged. "It isn't mine. I just use it where it's needed. Right now it's needed here."

"What if they decide to cross you? There's a price on your head, too."

He grinned. "Harder to collect, though. It's been tried before, by a couple of thousand dead men. You might point that out. This way is surer and richer. Think you can sell the package?"

"Sure I can sell it," she declared confidently. "I just hope some of the buyers can deliver."

Bolan produced a manila envelope from the cache behind the panel. "Here's your front money. Spread

120

it around, but watch out for the con artists and hang onto your purse. Those streets in the Quarter are already chaos and getting worse by the hour. Do business with no one but the guys on that list. There'll be no double-teaming this time. You're on your own from start to stop. I'm going to be very busy elsewhere. Get yourself killed and I'll never forgive you."

She laughed nervously. "You really do care, don't you?"

" 'Course I care," he replied gruffly. "Listen, Toni —you've got one big thing going for you, and it's more than looks—it's looks with *class*. These boys respect class in a woman. All the others are simply broads, and they'd as soon break a coke bottle inside of them as not. You're different, so use that difference. Don't play coy with these boys or make suggestive remarks."

Her eyes fell. "I guess you did catch my little routine with Lanza."

"That was perfect for that time and place," he told her. "But not in this next situation. Lanza's a hood, but he's a hood with a bit of class, himself. These boys down here on the streets are animals. Don't give them the slightest reason to think that you're in their class. They'd eat you alive."

Bolan removed a delicate chain, with crucifix attached, from her neck.

"Do they hate Catholics, too?" she murmured.

He replied, "Most of them go to confession every week. Good Catholics, these boys, for ten minutes every week." He was adding a bull's-eye cross to the chain. "They fear God once in a while but they fear *this* all the time. Wear it where they can see it.

Don't over play it. They'll notice it and they'll get the message."

"More class," she said with an impish smile.

He put the chain around her neck, then left his hands at her shoulders as he hung a quick, light kiss on those sweet lips. "Stay hard," he muttered.

Both her hands went behind his head and she pulled him back aboard, holding him there in a warm mingling of life forces. He was aware of her heart thudding against him as the kiss lingered on.

Yeah . . . a stolen moment of human intimacy in a sea of savagery.

Bolan understood; he hoped that she did too. It was not a commitment of lovers—but a savoring of adventurers, adventuring. Life was precious, the kiss said. Life was good, sacred—not for throwing away on the trifles and minutiae of the scramble for survival.

Life was for living largely—even sometimes on the shores of death.

She released him when the moment had run its course. Eyes lowered, sighing, she told the man, "Okay . . . okay . . . I'm hard."

16: SCRAMBLED

Bolan dropped Toni Blancanales a block away from where she'd left her car, sending her out among the wolves with a gentle pat on the shoulder. He felt uncomfortable about allowing her into the action—but she had a blood right, she was a professional, and his instincts trusted her ability to take care of herself.

Women were, after all, a hell of a lot more competent in such matters than most men would admit. And this woman was exceptional.

He'd known a few other exceptional women, of course—some of whom had not survived the game. But, then, he'd known some good men, also . . .

He dismissed this train of thought, clamping it off severely and wrenching his mind back to the problems of the battle for New Orleans.

Carlotti was hot; that much was certain. There had not been opportunity yet to check in on the Lanza episode—but Bolan knew without checking:

favorite son or no, Tommy Carlotti was at least under suspicion and now in deep trouble at the homestand.

A grin tugged at Bolan's lips as he played the scenario in his mind's eye. By now the word was probably out around town that the rackets cop, Jack Petro, had a bundle of hard evidence on Vannaducci's touchy financial entanglements. Petro's package, as of this time yesterday, had been Carlotti's package—homework assigned by a dying old *don* who wished only to turn the family business over to a beloved heir. Some heir. He'd have a sweet time explaining how he lost possession of the family's financial records. Especially on top of the surveillance intrigue with the financial boss, Lanza—who presented another interesting aspect to the race for power in New Orleans. Had Lanza known that the *capo* was schooling Carlotti in family business matters?

Carlotti was an inept, small-time hood. Bolan had known that from the beginning. The other bosses under Vannaducci must have known it also. Yeah, and there must be deep resentments there.

So, sure, Carlotti was on the hotspot.

Much more so than he could realize. Bolan knew something that the Boss of Sin did not know. His treachery had bought him nothing. Bolan had studied the campaign plan at army headquarters. And there was but one reading from it. In typical Mafia procedure, the turncoat had been assigned the task of fingering the top man for execution. Carlotti was supposed to "set up" old man Vannaducci for the St. Louis guns. What Carlotti did not know, but should have, was the other side of standard procedure: he was going to get it right along with the old man.

124

But now there was a development that was probably not yet known by the St. Louis guns. Their man Carlotti had become too hot to play the assassination game. And, unless Bolan's professional instincts were leading him completely astray, it seemed very likely that Tommy Carlotti was now lying low somewhere, hoping to avoid further compromise of his position and probably trying to figure some way to cool himself.

Bolan let his mind play with that situation as a familiarly icy sensation began spreading through his consciousness. Things were rapidly coming to a head in New Orleans, the boiling point very near. Typically, as that flash point approached, Bolan's own interior apparatus began taking on ice.

He did not enjoy these chess games with real men on the board of life and death.

But they were necessary.

And his mind was developing another scenario—a future one—as he again left the congested streets of the city behind him and sought a place with stretch. He found it in a shopping center in the northeast part of the city, where he parked the warwagon in an open area and went in search of a phone booth.

It was "dirty rat" time again. He did not consider it advisable to trust the moment to his mobile unit.

Moments later he was talking to the switchboard girl at the beachfront hotel in Mississippi. "This is urgent," he told her. "I have to talk to Mr. Stigni of the Midwestern Trade Group. I want you to drop everything and find him for me."

"Who's calling, please?" the operator asked nervously.

It wasn't exactly standard procedure for a hotel switchboard operator to inquire into the source of calls for guests—not even "urgent" calls. And the girl was too flustered. Bolan was betting his marbles on a police patch on that switchboard. He had, in fact, anticipated such an event.

"It's not important to you who's calling. It is to him. You tell him I'm on, and that I say he'd better *get* on. Do you understand me?"

"Yes, sir. One minute, sir."

The task required more than a minute; Bolan lit a Pall Mall and smoked it half away before the operator returned.

Her speech was stuttering a bit with the immensity of the moment as she reported, "I have him, sir. Just a moment. I'm ringing the other suite."

Bolan thanked her in a kindlier tone and counted the rings. Stigni came in on the sixth, although obviously he'd already agreed to take the call.

"Yeah, hullo, what the hell is this all about? Careful what you say, dammit, there's nosy ears everywhere."

"Eyes, too, Stigni," Bolan coldly assured him. "Ciglia there?"

"Who the hell is this?—*don't* say it right out!"

"Come on, you know my voice better than that—after all our jollies in the campaign room at noon. Put Ciglia on."

"Go to hell, you . . . ! You're *nuts!* I don't know no Ciglia! If you're talking about the poor man you took a shot at—"

Bolan's sense of sanity was struck by the ridiculous charade, the ludicrous insistence on anonymity at a time when every cop in the country knew by now who'd been shooting and who'd been shot at.

It was just another example of life in the Stone Age.

Grave situation or not, Bolan could not restrain himself from laughing in the guy's face. It was not a particularly joyful laughter, however, and the cold promise there shut Stigni down and left him spluttering.

Still chuckling, Bolan said, "Okay, forget Ciglia and put the 'poor man' on. I promise the phone isn't loaded, so I can't hurt him."

A coldly furious voice asked, "What are you trying to pull, guy?"

Sure, Ciglia'd been there all the while.

Bolan gave him a word. "Parley."

"After what you tried out here today?"

"Who was trying? I didn't have to go for the ball, you know. Just getting your attention."

"Okay, you got it. What do you want?"

"Stigni and I were discussing your campaign plans earlier today."

"That's a lie!" Stigni muttered from the background.

"So what?" Ciglia rasped. "We can always change the signals."

"You'd better. You've lost your inside track."

"Why should I be listening to this?"

"Because you know we have a mutual interest," Bolan replied. "And because you know I'm not just killing time."

"So what are you telling me?"

"Pack up and go home. Your strutting duck blew it. He's taken his final dive, and right now he's holed up somewhere just waiting for everybody to go away. The old man knows all, and he's got the dogs out."

"Wait a minute now. Let me see if I—you're saying our whole arrangement is shot. You're talking about our inside straight."

"That's it."

"Convince me."

"He won't be ordering any more shoes from Rome, Ciglia."

"I never said this was Ciglia."

It was a stall with the mouth, to allow the mind to catch up; Bolan knew that. He replied, "Wear whatever name you prefer. But wear it home. There's nothing left for you down here."

"Why're you being so kind to us, uh—Frankie, wasn't it? Why all the concern?"

Bolan said heavily, "You know how far my concern stretches for guys like you. I'll give it to you straight: I was hoping for you people to cancel each other out. But there's no way now—so why waste it? The old man's gone hard. His people are getting ready to disperse all around the Quarter. And he's got fifty to sixty braves wardancing around the River Road homestand. Your timing would backfire on you, the way things are now. Mardi Gras will be your largest problem instead of the cover you'd expected. The streets of the Quarter are choked with people right now—and it's getting worse, not better, all the way through tomorrow night. Pack up and go home, Ciglia. You'll be just one of the millions jamming these streets, with nobody around to fight. The home guard will lay low in the crowds and come out on Ash Wednesday to cut you in your sleep—or the next Wednesday or the Wednesday after that."

The chief of the war party was thinking that over —Bolan's logic had struck sensitive soil. Following an overlong silence, Ciglia replied, "How do you know so much?"

"I stay alive by knowing. How do you manage?"

"Don't get cute," the guy growled. "I still don't get *your* angle. Why the big sell?"

"It's no sell. Do what you please. I do have an interest, sure. But not that much."

"What's the interest?"

The guy was trying to probe Bolan now.

The Executioner's voice took on another layer of ice as he replied to that. "The old man will make an ass of you. He'll go from ashes to hero, overnight. I don't want that. I want him out."

"Well, so do we," Ciglia said, a bit of oil entering the voice now. "Maybe we should talk about that. Mutual interests, like you say."

"The line's still open and I'm still here," Bolan told him.

"Okay. Suppose for the moment that we do back off. What will you be doing?"

"I won't be backing off, Ciglia."

"No?"

"No."

"Oh, well, in that case . . . maybe you're right," Ciglia said sarcastically. "Maybe we should've just *stayed* home. Of course, we didn't know at the time that such a *hot* shot was coming in to clear the territory for us."

"Doesn't usually work that way, Ciglia. I'm a waster, not a builder. I don't clear territories. I close them down."

"You really are a hot shot, aren't you?" the guy snarled.

"I try to be. Well. Never say the man didn't warn you. You're now wearing the mark of the beast, Ciglia. Next time you step into my crosshairs, I won't be shooting at golf balls and bodyguards. Go home. Grow up. Live long. Goodbye."

Bolan hung up to a dead silence, a somber smile working at his lips but not quite reaching eye level.

A guy like Ciglia could not take that kind of talk.

He'd be roaring into New Orleans with all guns bared—maybe before the sun set again.

So . . . Bolan owed equal time to the other side. He settled the overtime charges with the long-distance operator, moved to another phone at the far end of the shopping center, and sent a probe into old man Vannaducci's sanctum sanctorum.

17: FLUSHED

A pleasantly modulated male voice responded to the first ring. "Mr. Van's office, Zeno here. Who's calling?"

"It's not Avon," Bolan told Zeno.

"Who is this? Where'd you get this number? Don't you know you're not supposed to—?"

Bolan said, "Relax, Zeno. I got the number from Tommy."

The line went momentarily dead. Bolan heard another extension lifting off. Then Zeno's cautious tones, "Is Tommy there? Put him on."

"He's not here," Bolan said. "I thought he was there."

"He's not here," Zeno shot back. "If he's not there, where is he?"

It was beginning to sound like an Abbot & Costello routine.

Bolan said, "Hell, I thought he was there."

"Who *is* this?" Zeno hissed.

131

"I'm tired of talking to you," Bolan said chattily. "You don't make sense. Is that you on the extension, Marco?"

"What the hell is going on here?" an older voice rumbled through the connection.

"Call it a demonstration. Shows how fouled up things can get when people play dumb games with who's who. Take Tommy, now. This morning. When he came driving in there with a short fuse wired to his foot. If he'd just told you, then and there, that he'd surrendered those ledgers to me, then maybe you could have taken some action to get them back. But it's too late for that now. You still there, Marco?"

"I'm here." The voice was suddenly tireder, heavier, much older. "This can be only one smart guy. Is that you?"

"It's me."

"Why're you calling me like this?"

"Did you know about the ledgers?"

"I been hearing words. Is it true?"

"It's true," Bolan said. "And I have some more words for you to live by, Marco."

"Why?"

"Call it a basic respect for senior citizens—or senior aliens, it makes no difference. I hear that Italy gets very sunny this time of year. Nice place to retire to, good place to die quietly."

"Smart guy!"

"Smarter than you, Marco. I know your family better than you do."

For some reason the old man was hanging in there, holding his temper—and now he was shifting the subject of conversation. "Is it true about Mississippi? That it's a St. Louis crew?"

"It is. Leading the charge is one of the young Turks, guy named Ciglia. I hear he's got visions of a throne of his own on the River Road estate. They'll be here tonight."

"How do you know that?"

"I was down there."

"Yeah, I heard something about that."

"Here's something I bet you haven't heard. They have an inside man here, deep in the pocket. He thinks he's going to set you up for them. Tomorrow, during the grand festivities."

"Baloney! I don't believe that! Why should I believe you?"

"Don't, then. But I could tell you who, when, where, and how."

"So tell," Vannaducci growled.

"You're the guest of honor for a Mardi Gras party tomorrow. Right? Tommy Carlotti's party. You'll be on his balcony overlooking the parade route when King Krewe passes by. Fill me in, Marco—I've never been to Mardi Gras. What is it like? Hysteria in the streets? Thousands and thousands of gay celebrants standing shoulder to shoulder and belly to buttock—music and frolicking and chaos as far as the eye can see? You lucky ones who have a balcony above that insanity—it presents a spectacle for you to boggle the mind, doesn't it? The parade—aw, the parade, that's something else. Lots of floats? Bands, marchers, hoopla? Confetti and streamers filling the air? These guys on the floats throw stuff to the crowd, don't they? Dubloons? You know something, Marco, one of those costumed clowns is going to reach right up onto Carlotti's balcony with a bag of dubloons that are not dubloons. Then . . . bang! Goodbye,

133

Marco. Or so Tommy thought. Instead it will be bang! bang!—goodbye Marco *and* Tommy!"

The telephone line was silent for a long moment. Presently, then, Zeno's smooth tones: "Mr. Van—regardless of who's telling it, it sounds right. It fits the other—"

"Shut up, Zeno!" the old man roared. "Don't you know who this smart guy is?"

"Save it, Marco," Bolan said. "I know more about what's happening here than both of you. I never enjoyed playing with an old man's heart—even a rotten old man like you, Marco—but your little golden heir is tin-plated, a forty-carat phony. He's been playing fast and loose with the keys to your kingdom for a long time now. He and Campenaro have been like streetcars between here and New York, setting this thing up."

"They couldn't put something like that together," the old man wheezed. "They ain't got it in them. I know Tommy's been doing something kinda off center, but I—"

"Is that what you built an empire on, Marco—wishful thinking? You ready to stake your life on it? Okay. Forget all this. I'll call Ciglia and tell him you refuse to believe a word of it. Then I'll get out of town and leave you alone. I won't be needed here after that. You go on to Tommy-boy's party, and you sit on that balcony and watch the festivities. *I'll* go to Italy and read your obituary under the Riviera sun."

"Wise guy," Vannaducci said tiredly.

Bolan went out on a limb of conjecture. "As for that job on Lanza—that was pretty rotten, wasn't it?

Aside from Zeno there, Lanza's the only worthwhile thing you have left in this town."

"Whatta you talkin' about?"

"You know what I'm talking about. Tommy's New York friends didn't trust your books, Marco—the ones you gave to Tommy. Sure—he made a copy and ran it right up. But they had to be sure you weren't leading their boy astray. That's why they wired Lanza up that way."

"Hey, guy. You think I'm a stupid old man, eh? You think I'm just going to take all this like from the goodness of your heart for me, eh?"

"There's a way you can check it out, Marco."

"Yeah? What way is that?"

"Tommy's taken a powder, hasn't he? You haven't been able to contact him since early this morning. You've just been hovering over that telephone all day, waiting for him to call in and settle this thing. Right?"

"Aaagh! You call that proof? How do I know he ain't laying dead in some ditch somewhere? Or maybe tied up in some crummy motel room while you play games with the old man, huh?"

"There's still a way to check it out."

"So tell me then."

"On my mother's sacred grave, Vannaducci, here's the way the thing lays out. Carlotti posed as a guy named Kirk from the—"

"Yeah I heard that story already!"

"It's straight, Marco. He conned a private investigation outfit into wiring Lanza for sound—an outfit called Able Group. The guys became suspicious and refused to turn the system over. Carlotti's got them on ice somewhere right now—alive or dead—I'd

135

guess dead, but there's always that chance you could turn them up alive. You'd know how to go about that better than I would. But if they *are* alive, Marco—well, they could have an interesting story for your ears. Look at it this way: they could clear the thing up, one way or another."

"I don't get you, Bolan. Why're you doing this? I know how you work. You're just trying to screw us up, get us to fighting each other. I know why you're doing this."

"Sure, I'll admit that. But I didn't do the screwing, Marco. That's just the way it is. Now you're damned if you act and you're doubly damned if you don't. Personally, for what it's worth, I'd rather see you out of it. You practically are already, anyway. You know that, so let's be men. Why fight it? Nothing that's left is worth it. There's nothing but bonepickers and jellyfish left of your family. And you can't take the empire into the grave with you, Marco. Take Zeno and get out. Go away. Lanza can shift for himself; he's gotten fat enough off of you as it is."

"You think I'm just gonna get up and walk away, eh?"

"I'll give you this much, Marco. A white flag until eight o'clock. You have that long to just get up and walk away. After that I'll forget that you're old and sick. I *won't* forget all the rotten misery you've brought to this place. I'll cancel you, Marco. I'll cancel you with all the rest."

A receiver clicked.

Zeno's voice, subdued and whispery, asked, "You say the St. Louis crowd is coming in tonight?"

Bolan replied, "Yeah. With more than a hundred

136

hard guns. They know their thing is busted now, so they're coming for a hot war."

"I don't know why you're doing this, Bolan, but —thanks."

"Don't thank me, guy. If you're there when I get there, I'll cancel you, too."

Bolan hung up, stared solemnly at the telephone for a moment, then mentally crossed his fingers and returned to the warwagon.

Vannaducci, he knew, would never "just get up and walk away."

The old man could not, of course, let on—right in Bolan's face—that he was buying the story of Carlotti's treachery.

But Marco Vannaducci was no idiot. Old, yes— sick, sure—dying, probably—threatened from every side, hell, yes. But he was still a highly dangerous old dog. He'd learned the infighting the hard way, and survived it, and built an empire on it.

He would be scrambling now, fast and hard. There would be hot blood in the Quarter today.

And maybe—just maybe—a couple of old friends from Able Team would get shook loose in the tumult, after all.

18: JUMP OFF

Mack Bolan knew a bit more about Jack Petro than the reverse case, and that was by no mere accident. He'd been interested in the cop since early on into this Southern expedition. The youngish cop's official life was more a matter of public record than that of the usual city detective—mainly due to his work with the New Orleans Crime Commission.

Petro had a law degree, but he had never bothered to sit for the state bar exam. He'd gone from college directly into law enforcement, first for a brief stint with the FBI in a small, western office. Dissatisfied with that duty, he'd served (again briefly) as a congressional staff investigator, then moved on to a job in his home state as a special investigator for the Louisiana state police. He lasted for two years there before settling finally for a detective's badge with NOPD.

He was regarded as brilliant, innovative—and a pain in the neck to some of the old-line cops who still believed that effective law enforcement was a routine matter of "roust, bust, bash, and belabor." Petro took a more aesthetic approach, working toward what he called "overview into the web"—he was, said the others, a correctional officer, not a cop.

Organized crime seemed a natural niche for a guy like Petro. But even the cops in that division found the "overeducated badge" a bit difficult to work with at times. When the spot opened, Petro was shunted into a sort of autonomous office as liaison officer with the Crime Commission, a civilian outfit with powers to investigate, report, and recommend—but not to actually enforce the law.

Jack Petro had been in the office ever since. He'd "banged on the walls" all over that town, then the state, then at various points around the country—as a speaker and professional witness before other commissions, legislative and congressional committees, and as an expert witness in a number of federal courtrooms.

Yeah, Bolan knew a lot about Jack Petro. Even the vital statistics: age thirty-three, married to a lovely Creole childhood sweetheart, two small children, Catholic, Democrat.

Bolan had sensed something special about the guy even before that first telephone conversation.

It was now time to put that "sensing" to the test. He boldly called the cop from his mobile phone in the warwagon and told him. "This is Bolan. I figured I owed you a call."

"I figured the same thing," Petro replied tartly. "That's why I've been holed up here all day waiting for it."

Bolan said, "I hear you got the package."

"I did. Thanks. Couple more like that and I'll be out of a job again. Where are you, Bolan?"

"Just cruising your town, Petro. You were right, it's crowded. I was wrong—there *will* be gunplay in the streets. I'd like to minimize it. How about you?"

The cop seemed a bit dazed by it all. "Minimize? Me? Oh, sure, 'course I would. What, uh, do you have, uh, in mind?"

"Ciglia and the St. Louis guns are probably headed this way by now. More than a hundred of them. And I'm getting worried about that. There's no room for them on these streets. You reading?"

"Yeah. The figures we got from Mississippi, though, read more like about fifty guns."

"Wrong. That doesn't include street talent recruited on the spot in Mississippi. They'll be coming in a hundred strong and more. I also have some intelligence to the effect that a special supercharged head squad came down from New York to help quarterback the play. That probably means a convoy. I saw a lot of big, shiny limousines in that parking lot on the beach. Shouldn't be hard to spot and track if they do come in convoy. There's, uh, just no damn room downtown here for those people. That's all I have to say about that."

"Sure, I get you. You're sure about this, now?"

"Reasonably sure. Actually it's my fault. I wanted to egg them in here before the grand hoopla of tomorrow. I'd have never expected this place to grow so wild in just the past few hours. Will it keep growing at this rate?"

"It will," Petro replied, sighing.

"Okay. End of subject. Here's a new one. I need a favor. Maybe you're my man."

140

The cop coughed and replied, "Run it by. We'll see how it fits."

Bolan quickly and succinctly related the story about Able Group, complete to present time except for the true identity of the missing men. Petro listened with interest, occasionally breaking in with questions and comments. Bolan wound up the tale by adding, "The young lady is out working the streets right now. When and if she makes a positive contact, I'd like to designate you as go-between."

Petro sat silent over that for a moment, then: "You want me to handle the ransom, to pay it if all conditions are met."

Bolan said, "That's right."

"Why me?"

"I trust you. The matter is, uh, very close to me."

"Okay. When and where do we get together?"

"Money will be in your office within an hour. That's as close as you and I are likely to get."

The cop chuckled. It was a strained, brittle sound. "I'm going to get fired. Did you know that? Never mind—don't say anything. I'm sick of the damn walls, anyway. Listen to me, Bolan. This tip on the St. Louis guns—did you drop that on me with the expectation that I'd pass it along to the right people?"

Bolan chuckled and replied, "I figure you for a good cop, Petro."

"So where does that leave you? I have a tip for you, phone pal. A contingent of hotshot state troopers are already on the problem. They're not going to jump those people at the state line, you know. They're going to move in right with them, very quiet and very close, and they'll wait for an incrim-

141

inating event before another move is made. When they close on them, chances are they'll be closing on you as well. Have you considered that?"

"I have."

"Don't push your luck, chum. I may not always agree with my peers on police methodology, but let me give it to you straight. These cops down here are not clowns. They're damn tough and they play for keeps."

Bolan said, "I hope so. This guy Ciglia is as hard as they come. Have you run a make on him?"

"Sure. He's pulled everything in the book. No convictions. I get the idea Missouri would love to see him gone for good. Very bad character. We sure as hell don't want to inherit him."

"Maybe you can bury him for the state of Missouri. One more thing, Petro. You know the town and the people. If you were Tommy Carlotti—with everybody in town after your ass—where would you drop down to cool it off?"

The rackets cop thought about that for perhaps ten seconds before replying, "I'd go to my secret honey's pad over on Dauphine. Is he that hot?"

"Yeah. Is she that secret?"

"She is. Local socialite and widow who must think it's terribly exciting to bed down with a common hood. I happen to know the lady through a club my wife belongs to."

"I'm surprised Carlotti wouldn't brag up a connection like that," Bolan mused.

"It's a mixed bag. Carlotti's a punk, sure. But he also has very strong survival instincts. Maybe he's been looking ahead to just this sort of possibility. I do know that the whole thing is very hush-hush.

I've even kept it out of my reports because of the lady involved. I mean, what the hell, what would be served by publishing that sort of garbage?"

"I need that address, Petro."

"Why?"

"I'll try not to embarrass the lady. But she could be in big trouble. I know for a fact that Carlotti is. Give me the address."

Petro reluctantly parted with the information, then said: "What the hell is this, Bolan? It's been like dreamtime all day long around here. What kind of cop sits and chats, exchanging tidbits with the most wanted fugitive in the country? What kind of fugitive—?"

Bolan cut him off with a flat chuckle. "I heard a one-liner on the radio the other night to fit that, Petro. Something about . . . a life is meant to be composed like a song—from the heart, with instinct and compassion—not copied in block type from a book of rules."

"Sure," was Petro's only comment to that.

"Live large, Jack."

"Sure, sure."

Bolan broke the connection there and turned his attention to the more pressing problems of the day.

There was going to be hell in these streets.

That much was certain.

Bolan's own orchestration of events had assured that. The only consolation for the man was the certain knowledge that it would have been far worse if allowed to develop under its own head of steam. The streets were impossible today; they would be insane tomorrow.

This way, at least, Bolan could exert some handle

on the situation; it would be possible to minimize the risks to innocent bystanders.

But the insanity was already setting in. The streets of the Quarter were absolutely nonnegotiable for vehicular traffic. Nothing was moving on wheels in there but paddy wagons, emergency vehicles, and booze supply trucks. You couldn't *clear* those streets with a team of bulldozers. There was no way to remove the people. And the activities would not dwindle here with the appproach of night; they would heighten, and keep building without letup until the big climax tomorrow night.

Fat Tuesday, yeah.

Fat *chance* for containing an overflow of violence in the streets if the gunplay should be allowed to coincide with the hours of peak insanity.

So, yes—he'd played it right. Now he had to get it all on the numbers, tightly cadenced and moving along under his command.

No easy job, that. Hell, no. But whoever said that any of it was supposed to be easy? *Easy* was not the name of the game. The name was *knockout!* Not a TKO, either. They had to be beaten to the flat of their backs, bloodied and senseless, then buried under their own weight without allowing any seepage to ringside.

So okay. Okay. Once more around the town, then— with eyes and ears wide open and fully extended—a final sizing for the climactic battle for New Orleans.

The big kill was on.

Petro turned to his friend from State and said, with a wry smile, "Well . . . you heard. What d'you say?"

144

The state investigator raised both shoulders in an exaggerated shrug. "Sounds like a cool guy. But you shouldn't forget what side of the law he's on. He's dynamite, buddy, pure dynamite."

"You'd better call your people," Petro muttered.

State sighed and reached for the telephone.

Dreamlike, sure, Petro was thinking. Worse than that—almost like a long-running *déjà vu.* What a day! And it was getting wilder by the minute. The reports filtering up from the sources on the streets were telling of wild men running around everywhere —all through the Quarter and down along the Market—up and down Canal Street—over into the Irish Channel and even up into the Garden area. The search, no doubt, for Bolan's friends—a frantic treasure hunt, with Lieutenant Jack Petro of NOPD now holding the payoff bag.

Talk about dissolving walls!

Other reports hinted at growing dis-ease and unrest among the known crime element in and around the city. Sporadic shootings and assaults, in a seemingly unconnected sequence, but all involving the same element—certainly indicative of growing tensions and flaring tempers as the sides squared off and battle lines began drawing their web about the city.

Minimize it? Jack Petro could not even *comprehend* it! How the hell could a guy like Bolan—a lone guy—under fire from all sides at once and with nothing approaching the resources of a police organization—how the hell could a guy in that position hope to get a handle on it?

Still . . . Petro felt that, by God, the guy *would!*

The man from State was having trouble getting a line through the switchboard. Petro surged to his feet, looked around the office as though perhaps he might never see it again, then told his friend, "Stay with it, wallbanger. If I'm not back in a reasonable time . . . notify my next of kin, huh?"

"Where you going?"

"I think it's time I put this all on the line. I'm going up to talk to the chief."

The man from State grinned worriedly. "Full disclosure?"

"Half full, anyway. My own department has a right to this stuff. Stay here, will you? If a little green man with pointed ears should pop in here with a bag of money, I want someone here to receive it. Okay?"

State grinned, "I might even offer him a drink."

"Make your call. Hurry, guy, hurry! The walls are crashing down everywhere—can't you hear them? Don't miss your piece of the action."

The guy was laughing as Petro stepped through the doorway . . . but it was clear that he did not know why.

Jack Petro knew why.

Humpty Dumpty banged on a wall.

The wall fell but Humpty didn't.

My, what a view! The wall, now, isn't!

The ex-wallbanger from C/C Liaison chuckled fitfully all the way to the chief's office.

19: CRUSHED

A harried and unbelieving cop on horseback charged across the intersection, a moving black hole in the churning sea that scattered as if on signal, as he yelled in at Bolan, "Hey, you can't take that bus through here! What the hell do you—back that goddam thing around and get it the *hell* out of here!"

Bolan stuck an arm out the window to wave a clipboard with an impressive looking sheaf of papers clamped to it. "Television mobile unit," he yelled back. "Read the permits, dammit. I'm going through!"

"*Read?* Are you nuts, *read?* Awright, go on! Don't squash any more loonies than you have to!"

"How 'bout clearing a path for me?"

"Oh, sure! What should I do—throw horse shit at them? Get outta here, go on! Just sit on your horn and go!"

Bolan did so.

Ten minutes later he'd managed to creep the fifty or so feet desired to make it into the shallow recess of a recently burned building in the very heart of the French Quarter.

An all-black marching band in dizzying uniforms was marking time right outside his window while continuing a piercing recital of "Basin Street Blues."

The intersection and the mounted cop, just fifty feet back, seemed swallowed and lost forever in the depths of the past.

Someone tossed a candy sucker through the window. Bolan waved to the anonymous giver in the sea of faces and clamped the sucker between his teeth, then he closed the window and set the locks.

If it wasn't Mardi Gras yet, he was damned glad it wasn't.

Other vehicles were creeping through the chaos, horns blaring incessantly—one, a beer truck, the object of tumultuous attention by the crowd surrounding it just a few yards ahead. The brass band was stuck behind the truck, and the truck was bogged down completely now by a human wave that clung to every inch of its body.

Another black hole was moving down the street toward the besieged vehicle, on a mission of rescue.

This was something a person had to experience to believe.

Bolan shook his head and stepped outside, to the lee side of madness. He'd wedged his wagon into the recess in such a manner that no vehicle could flow around the starboard flank. He went to the rear and fired up the auxiliary generator, simply for the sake of realism, then he grabbed a couple of dummy power cables and spread them along the length of the vehicle. It didn't have to make sense; it just had to be there.

A couple of large decals quickly affixed to the windows completed the job of cosmetic security; the warwagon was now a television network "Mardi Gras Mobile Unit."

And the Executioner had himself a forward base, in the heart of the synthetic madness that was "the Quarter at Carnival."

Day was fading quickly; night edging in and bringing with it an entirely new tenor to the revelries.

Bolan stepped over an empty bottle of Boone's Farm Apple Wine and went back inside.

He stripped down to the blacksuit and carefully selected weaponry for the hard probe into Tommy Carlotti's possible hideaway.

He chose the AutoMag, without backup—loose cartridges in the pocket instead of spare clips—then he went out to join the insanity.

The whole damn town was in costume for Carnival.

And so was Bolan.

The French Quarter of New Orleans is a quaint old section that actually embodies the romance and much of the historic culture of the city. Narrow streets designed originally for men on horseback form canyons between unbroken lines of storefronts and row-houses, many of these latter rising three or more stories high and featuring balconies projecting over the street.

The contrast between "outside" and "inside" French Quarter can often be startling for the unsuspecting visitor. Aged and decrepit facades lining the narrow and usually dirty streets may conceal breathtaking splendor within—and such was the case with the address on Dauphine Street.

Even the facade here seemed less seedy dressed in the festive trappings of Carnival—but it was still weathered wood and sagging balconies to the outside eye. An enclosed courtyard fronted on the street, secure and private behind a stucco wall, exclusive by virtue of a high wooden gate and two big black dudes costumed like Zulu warriors and standing guard over the invitation list.

The balconies here hung out over the courtyard rather than the street. A party was underway in there—may have been for days—and the merry sounds from within were spilling forth to mingle with and sometimes overcome the less concerted sounds of the street. All three stories were brightly lighted, and Bolan could see costumed folk here and there on a wrought-iron stairway that apparently rose from the courtyard to the decorated balconies above.

He decided against a bluff at the gate or at the front door, electing instead to allow himself to be carried along with the ever-moving crowd along Dauphine, then around the corner. From there he found the back way in, going up and over the top of an adjacent structure, then onto the roof of the target area.

From that point, it was apple pie.

He swung down off the roof and onto a third-floor balcony overlooking the courtyard, stood in the shadows up there for a brief visual orientation, then went inside to comparative silence.

The heart of the party was obviously down below in the open area, fifty or sixty costumed revelers milling around with drinks held high, talking and laughing and having a grand time.

A small musical group off to one corner was hardly heard above the overall sound of the party itself, and there was certainly nowhere to dance.

Bolan had hardly entered the premises before he was struck by a definitely off-key atmosphere—a tingling sensation in the hairs of his nose and a lifting of instinctive hackles.

This place was a hellground!

That was not an intellectual judgment, but a certain knowledge borne by soul-shaking experiences in similar arenas.

He followed his quivers, as augmented by an almost imperceptible odor to which he had long ago become sensitized—that sickening *turkey odor*—and he located the source of it all in a small storage room set into the stairwell between the second and third floors.

It was Blancanales and Schwarz.

But they were not turkeys, yet—not quite.

They sat half-upright on the floor, hands and feet tied together, backs slumped and twisted against the wall.

Their clothing was impregnated with a mixture of dried blood and vomit, soaked with fresh sweat, urine, and probably everything else that could be squeezed from a living body and yet leave it living.

There was fresh blood, also, from a fresh kill that lay twisted between them. Both were conscious but barely aware; neither had found the strength or perhaps the need to move aside from the burdening corpse of a local buttonman whom Bolan immediately recognized as one of Carlotti's runners.

Bolan pulled the little guy clear and went to work on his friends, cutting bonds and carefully massaging long-restricted circulation.

Both of Schwarz's eyes were swollen shut; the entire face was a swollen, pulpy mass from repeated beatings.

Blancanales was in better shape, but not much; at least he could move glinting eyes around the swollen sockets and find room to extend a bloated tongue between caked dry lips.

"God's sake, Pol!" Bolan groaned.

"Okay, I'm okay. Sarge, he . . ." The voice faded beyond perception, choked off by dried and swollen tissues.

"Yeah, Pol—*what!*—say it again!"

"He—God!—he's got Toni."

"*Who* has her?"

"Kirk. Jus' now, minute ago. She . . . came to get us." Those eyes flickered toward the wall. "Li'l guy there. Kirk shot 'im, took Toni."

Bolan growled, "Hang tight! I'll be back!"—and he hit that doorway running.

Spotting a guy like Carlotti in that festive variety of costumed figures would have been next to impossible; *not* to spot *Toni*—in any crowd—was just as impossible.

They were headed up the outside stairway, climbing for the third-floor balcony—Carlotti dragging the girl along beside him.

Bolan sprung the AutoMag and threw the big .44 to full extension across that short right angle to doomsday as he cried out, "Car-*lotti!*"

The guy froze in a half turn, a big pistol filling

152

his own paw, to gaze back for perhaps a heartbeat on the collector of mortgaged souls.

It could have been a fair contest—gun to gun, damn near toe to toe—but the big little man who would wear no shoes but elevators from Rome was not up to a man-sized response to the challenge of life or death. Instead, he elected to cut bait, jamming the pistol against Toni's head and screaming, "Stay away from me, Bolan—*stay away!*"

Bolan stayed away.

He wouldn't have touched that guy with someone else's hands.

The AutoMag, however, had a mind of its own. It roared out fire and massive disgust, hurling 300 grains of splattering death crashing through that collapsing skull in a path from ear to ear, leaving not even a dying reflex to carry out the threat to the girl.

The guy was dead before the gun slipped from his grasp, the liberated soul shrieking out across the expanses of hell before the body caught on to what had become of the head.

The remains toppled and wedged between steps and railing.

Toni staggered against the balustrade with the soft moan, "Oh, God."

There is a particular quality to the sound of a heavy pistol in discharge, a report that batters the air and flails the ears for yards around—but not even that was enough to immediately seize the attention of the partygoers in the courtyard, just below. It was a slow, domino-type reaction—with first one mind and then another lifting to a perception of that which had occurred, to the sobering spectacle of violent death hanging above and dripping blood into the party.

A woman down there shrieked—then another—and suddenly the party was over, the revelry gone, only the sounds from the street lifting like a returning echo into the sudden silence of the moment.

Bolan had snared Toni and snatched her back beneath the protection of the second-floor porch. Now he gazed down on the crowd, AutoMag still bared, and called down to them: "Everyone go home, get out of here. The place could be a shooting gallery in a matter of minutes."

Someone down there laughed drunkenly, but another was sober enough to note, "Hell, he's serious."

"That's Mack Bolan!" a man's awed voice observed.

Never had a Carnival party broken up so fast, so quietly, and so completely. One moment they were all there, gazing up at him with a mixture of horror and fascination; the next, they were all gone—most of them out through the gates and past the dumbfounded "Zulu" watchmen, some fading silently indoors and out through the house, Bolan supposed.

Toni was working hard at getting it back together. She stammered, "Mack I—I found—I f-found—"

He said, "I know. They'll be okay, Toni. Get to the phone. Call the police. Ask for Petro—Lieutenant Jack Petro. Tell him what's here. We need an ambulance, and we need it screaming."

"I—I..."

"You can. Do it now. Then stay with the guys until help arrives. No matter what. Understand? No matter *what!*"

"What... is happening?"

"Bloody Monday is happening. I expect—"

154

What Bolan "expected"—as a result of his final city recon—had already arrived. Four energetic hardmen came through that gate down there, shoving the watchmen in ahead of them.

Then Richard Zeno stepped in.

Bolan gave the girl a shove and hissed, "Now!"

Haunted eyes turned back to give him a final flicker of understanding and gratitude; then she was gone.

He moved back to the stairway and called down, "You're late, Zeno. Party's over."

Five sets of eyes lifted to that outstretched .44, but not a hand so much as quivered.

Zeno yelled, "You can't take us all, Bolan!"

"I don't want you all, not right now. I got what I came for. I believe it's the same thing you wanted. I'm offering you a white flag to take it the hell out of here."

"You've got Tommy?"

"What's left of him, yeah."

"Send it down."

Bolan did so, using a foot to nudge and guide the limp remains to the edge and over. The body hit the courtyard and bounced, limbs flopping in the recoil like a rag doll.

Without sound or sign, the hardmen bent backs to the task, bore up their ex-heir apparent and unceremoniously hauled him away, a man to each lifeless limb.

Zeno followed them out, pausing at the gate to lift an impassive face to the man on the stairway; then he too was gone.

A moment later Bolan heard the telltale sounding

of the horn as the limousine began working its way through the crowd.

In a way, it was sad. Not the death of an animal like Tommy Carlotti. But the death of an old man's dream—even a savage old man like Marco Vannaducci.

Bolan turned away from that moment and went inside.

Bloody Monday had not ended.

It had just begun.

20: BURIED

Bolan remained with his friends, lending all assistance and comfort possible under the circumstances, until the commotion of the emergency vehicles joined the other sounds outside. Then he made a quick and quiet farewell and went out the way he'd come—across the rooftops.

He returned to the warwagon for a brief reselection of weapons, loading up for heavy combat and returning immediately to his rooftop highway. He used that super highway in the sky for most of ninety minutes, traversing the entire district from sector to sector and grid to grid—seeking the Stone-Agers, finding them, executing them, then moving immediately on to the next preselected target of the chase.

Not once was he challenged by the law, and only twice did he encounter pitched-battle resistance from among those marked for death.

They were mostly small-timers and gun soldiers

—the flotsam and jetsam of the New Orleans crime world who were not considered important enough or worthy enough for saving by a besieged *capo*. They were expendables. Bolan spent them.

The only fish of any consequence left behind was Enrico Campenaro—and this time a Vannaducci crew apparently got there first. The overambitious and turncoat enforcer would have fared far better under Bolan's cleansing wind. His former *amici* had drawn and quartered him, beheaded him, and left the dripping head perched atop a small fishbowl like a grinning Mardi Gras devil—to drain.

Bloody Monday, yeah, and Bolan was sick of the smell of it when he returned finally to his forward base, broke camp, and set horn-tooting sail upon that sea of human joy. Hardly a hair of Carnival had been disturbed by the bloodletting in its midst.

Bolan could not speak for the revelers; he himself, though, was ready for Ash Wednesday and the thirty-nine meatless days to follow.

Bloody Monday was not, however, done with Mack Bolan yet.

As soon as he had worked his way clear of Carnival, Bolan punched in his mobile phone and leaned once again on the law.

Petro responded immediately with the opening line: "I hope it's you."

"It is," Bolan replied tiredly. "It's mostly done, down here. What's the reading on the kidnap victims?"

"They'll make it. Starved, dehydrated, tortured beyond ordinary endurance—but the medics say they're going to be okay, unbelievable as it may have seemed an hour or so ago. Hardly any lasting effects except for the big fella, Morales—or whatever name you're running him as—he, uh, may have permanent loss of hearing in one ear. Also a kidney took a lot of damage—could lose that if it doesn't begin functioning. I think they're both lucky as hell and so do they. Uh, the young lady is . . ."

"Is what?"

"In love, I'd guess, with a certain fugitive who doesn't really have a damn thing to offer her. Sad, isn't it? Love means walls."

Bolan said, "She'll survive it."

"So will I, but this all leaves me with an embarrassing problem."

"Just one?" Bolan asked.

"One in particular. The damn ransom package. Who earned it?"

"A dead man. Pay his estate."

"What estate? The poor shit doesn't even have a legal name that anyone will admit to knowing. Turns out, by the way, he was probably the only person in the world besides Carlotti who knew about the kidnapping. Not even the mistress of the prison household knew. She fainted just from the smell of that room. Those top floors have been closed off for years. I personally know that to be true."

"What was the little guy's connection to Carlotti?"

"Oh, hell, an errand boy. Hardly even spoke English, lived over in the old Spanish section. Your girl told me that he helped Carlotti tie them up, that's all. Never saw them again until tonight, and he was just working a hunch on the Dauphine address. He carried messages there for Carlotti from time to time."

"Toni's a pretty damn good detective," Bolan commented.

"Yeah. Well, the whole thing was a tragic, stupid . . ."

Bolan asked, "Anybody confirm the reason for the snatch?"

"Your men aren't up to saying much just yet. But apparently it was just about the way you laid it out for me. The guys never did like the setup. They balked at turning the operation over, especially after listening to their test tape. Carlotti panicked. Couldn't let them go, afraid they'd talk to the wrong people. Didn't want to scratch them without learning how to use the operation. He just couldn't admit to his own sponsors that he'd goofed up a very expensive operation. He was trying to beat the secret out of your guys. The lunatic. Left them tied up there, no food or water, sitting in their own piss and shit—aaagh! I don't know how or even why they held out. These, uh, guys . . . they're a bit more than just . . ."

"Leave it where it lies, Petro."

"I seem to remember hearing about a couple of—"

"Leave it there."

"Sure. That's all I was going to say. So what about this bag I'm left holding? That kind of money scares hell out of me. Don't leave it on my doorstep, guy."

"It isn't mine, Petro. It's Able Group funds."

"Oh. Oh, I see. Okay. I'll see that they get it back."

"Fine. Now let's discuss the nitty of the night. What has become of the Mississippi hardforce?"

"Well, they *were* causing a monumental traffic

160

problem up on the interstate. Squad of city cops met them as they were moving onto the Canal offramp. Told them, quite firmly, to back off and bug off. The town was full."

Bolan said, "City cops, eh?"

"Yeah. Led by our chief himself."

"How'd he know?"

"I told him. He about blew my head off with sheer lungpower, then took immediate steps to close the city to undesirables."

"You said something about a traffic jam."

"Yeah. Ciglia stood up there and orated like a consitutional lawyer for more than an hour. Trying to bluster his way through."

"When did they spring loose?"

"Just before you called."

"I see. Which way?"

"West. I, uh, hear they turned onto Airline Highway and dropped in on Jefferson Parish."

"South on Causeway?"

"Yeah. Or so I hear. River Road's down that way."

"So it is," Bolan said.

"Don't go."

"Why not? CID still tracking?"

"Just don't."

"May as well. Not much left in the city."

"You may be right about that. I hear that things are getting so bad down at the morgue that the incoming corpses are being asked to please take a number and have a seat. Sort of amazing, too."

"What's amazing?"

"Sudden contagion of head hits. You know, bullets in the ears, in the nose and mouth—all that certain death stuff. Some guy has been very busy in this town tonight."

"More than one guy, Petro," Bolan said tiredly. "Nobody retires gracefully from you know where. Marco's been purging the ranks, thinks he has things nailed down again. He's pared to the bone now, and I'd say drawing in tight. And, you know, he just might be stronger than ever."

"I don't think so," the cop replied quietly. "Way I've been hearing it, the golden empire is buried in the flames of Carnival—and it will not rise from the ashes of Wednesday. Not even forty days of Lent will bring it back."

"There's only one way to be sure of that," Bolan said.

"Your way, huh?"

"Yeah. My way."

"Don't go. You were close on that count. One hundred and twenty guns. Now *there's* a way. They'll take care of it for you."

"For themselves, maybe. It just grows a new head and springs back—and it doesn't even need ashes to rise from."

"Guess you're right," the cop said. "I can give you this. The books you donated will bury a lot of fat cats, too. In the, uh, you know, so-called legit community. They contribute to the problem, you know. Feed it, then feed themselves from the regurgitation. We'll nail them."

"Do that," Bolan said. "Keep on doing it."

"Wallbanging, you mean. Sure."

"Petro, you're a hell of a guy. Thanks for that."

"You too. Hang in tight, man—and watch those flanks."

162

"With both eyes," Bolan assured him, and broke away.

Sure, he'd be watching his flanks.

It was time to go for the knockout.

Old *Marco* wasn't buried yet.

21: ATTACK!

Sixteen shiny limousines with engines off and lights extinguished were lined bumper to bumper along the River Road fronting the Vannaducci estate. Another two had gone on down the drive to the security gate and were idling there, lights on, engines running.

Bolan read it as a parley—or as an attempt at one.

He sent the warwagon cruising slowly along the parked line of vehicles on River Road, using night-bright optics in a probe of their interiors.

The wheelmen were all there—bored, smoking. Also, in each car, sat one or two other hardmen. All told, maybe thirty to forty guns—but no more than that.

Those numbers did not compute.

Where the hell was the rest of the force?

Vannaducci would never invite that whole damn head party inside his security area—whatever the defensive strategy. Bolan had breached that security area himself, twice, on soft recon missions—and he knew where all the strength lay: on those defense perimeters. The heart of the estate was soft, not hard. No—it did not compute.

The atmosphere in the second floor study was tense, electric. The old man was on his "pacing track"—a small oval rug behind the desk. Frank Ebo sat on a forward corner of the desk, slumped, a telephone at his ear—but conversing with no one.

The only light in the room was coming from a small, muffled lamp on the back wall; much of the study was in semidarkness, as was that entire level of the house.

Algiers boss Harry Scarbo—a chubby little man with a round face and an unlighted cigar perpetually clamped between the teeth, stood at the draped front window with binoculars.

Rocco Lanza was pulling similar duty at a side window.

Zeno, accompanied by Ralph Pepsi and two machine-gun toting defenders of the manse, had gone to the gate for a parley with the New York delegation waiting there.

Vannaducci halted his pacing long enough to inquire of the room in general, "How many cars did you say out there?"

House boss Ebo screwed his head around to quietly reply, "At least fifteen, maybe more."

"That Bolan wasn't bullshitting us, was he?" the old man said worriedly, for perhaps the fifth time that evening.

165

Ebo shook his head and returned it to telephone duty.

"So what're they doing out there now, Harry?" Vannaducci yelled to Scarbo.

"Finished," the Algiers boss reported from the window. "Zeno's headed back. We got something new way out front, too—bus, whattaya call 'em, mobile—motor home."

"What the hell?" Ebo growled. "They bringing 'em down now by tour buses?"

Vannaducci scowled at his house boss. "Get that guy off the damned pot, will you."

Ebo shook the phone beside his head as he replied, "They've gone to get him, Marco. But it's going to be the same answer. They're all scared off. All these important friends—shit—listen, a time like this is when you separate the friends from the goats."

"We put 'im in office," Lanza commented, turning from the window to glare at Ebo as though it was all his fault. "He damn well better deliver something."

"Let's be realistic about that," Ebo muttered. "The heat's on. When the heat goes on, everybody goes indoors to cool off."

Vannaducci mumbled a string of obscenities and continued pacing.

Lanza was not satisfied. He took a couple of steps toward Ebo and growled, "Look, hang it up. He's not coming. Don't look like you're sitting there begging for crumbs. We'll return the favor to the smartass when things are different."

Ebo's gaze transferred to the *capo*. "Marco?"

"Yeah, hang it up. Call Florida."

"Jesus Christ!" Lanza exploded. "What good can Florida do at a time like this! This is Louisiana,

Marco—and those are New York hoods down there pounding on the gates!"

"I want some cops out there to clear that fuckin' street!" the old man roared back. "I pay my damn taxes, don't I? I give to the damn funds and the damn benefits and the damn campaigns, don't I? Now I want some damn service out here, and I want it quick!"

"Well, you're not going to get cops from Florida, Marco."

"You'd be surprised what I get from Florida, Rocco. Now get off my shoulders! Frank—you call Florida!"

The house boss was already initiating the call.

The despairing Lanza yelled, "Aw, shit, Marco!"

"Aw, shit, yourself!" the old man roared back. "Keep your eyes and ears open, kid, you might learn something around here tonight. What the hell you think moves things around this town—around any town? It's phone calls, that's what. A word here and a word there between friends, see. That's what it's all about!"

Harry Scarbo called back from his post at the front window, "That motor home is back again. Believe it's coming along the drive now. I can't—the damn trees, Marco, why you gotta have so many trees? It's, uh, a camper, I guess—yeah, a damn camper."

Eyebrows raised, Ebo commented, "They use those sometimes to—" He dropped his voice suddenly and pitched it into the telephone.

Vannaducci growled, "I don't care if they got—"

Zeno came puffing through the door to announce, without preliminaries: "That was no parley, Marco—it was an ultimatum. That's Alfred Damio down there. He says—"

Vannaducci interrupted with an observation of his own. "Sure—New York, by way of my late friend, Freddie Gambella. Well, well. How's Al?"

"I said an ultimatum, Marco. He's tough as nails and in no mood for renewing old acquaintances. He's carrying an invitation from you know where. Inviting you out, that is. Says it's all over for us here, Marco. Says it's a solid front in New York and they've decided it's time for the change. Says your replacement is here and waiting. Says—I"

Vannaducci yelled, "Whatta you mean talkin' to me like that!"

"It's not me, Marco. It's them."

"I mean them! They send a punk *messenger boy* to say something like that?"

"That's not all," the *consigliere* went doggedly on. "They're saying we have an hour to clear out. He's got a plane waiting for you, Marco."

"A *plane?* A plane for *where?*"

"Costa Rica," Zeno muttered.

"Aw, *shit* on them! Bunch o' damn punks—I *baptized* half o' them punks!"

A wild-eyed Ralph Pepsi ran in at that moment, sliding to a respectful halt and teetering on tiptoes just inside the door. Ebo dropped the phone to his chest and lifted questioning eyes to the youth. "What now?"

"They're coming toward the west wall! I sent some boys down to back up—"

"How many coming?"

"Can't tell! They say maybe twenty or thirty, on foot! I sent Pat's crew down to shore it up! Should I . . . ?"

Harry Scarbo had turned back to his post. He

yelled, "Jesus *Christ!*" at the same moment that a bright flash illuminated the night out there and a fairly close explosion puffed and rattled the glass of the window.

"*What's that?*" Vannaducci screamed.

"A cannon!" the stunned Algiers boss reported. "They got a damn *cannon* on that thing!"

The term "cannon"—in street parlance—usually refers to a handgun of impressive caliber. But Harry Scarbo had used the word in its literal sense, and he was not far from right.

Bolan's new warwagon came equipped with a bit more than mere electronic marvels. It was also something of a dreadnought on wheels, a rolling battleship with built-in firepower utilizing the latest and best lightweight armament this side of atomics. A rocket launcher was built into the roof, controlled from the driver's seat, and could be used while the vehicle was underway. A motorized, swivel-platform with a four-rocket capability retracted into a hatch on the roof for concealment during "soft" periods, rising and locking into firing position on command from a dashboard control.

Targeting was via electronic circuitry tied into the regular optics surveillance system, foot-controlled and fired from a floor-mounted fire control device that Bolan described in his journal as "a rock-and-press trackfire." A supple ankle and a steady foot were the only human requirements; no hands were needed.

Reloads were another matter. There was no reload capability in the heat of combat. It was a "four-shot system," and thus not to be used indiscriminately.

The vehicle was not armored, nor were the windows bulletproof. The "command chair" was, however, solid steel beneath the padding, and special protective panels were strategically placed inside the skin of the cab, these features affording a "better than nothing" shield for the driver.

Bolan had scouted the enemy task force and made a run along the front boundary of the Vannaducci estate, using the nightbright optic system. His readings of the situation there were fairly accurate, his attack a "seize the moment" maneuver played entirely by ear.

As his vehicle wheeled slowly onto the tree-lined drive leading to the main gate, it drew interested stares from the tail cars of the caravan but no challenges.

When halfway along that doomsday trail and into the final straightaway, he "enabled" the rocketry, a move that automatically switched the optics over to fire control, superimposing an electronic grid with range marks on the viewplate—confirmation that the launch platform had achieved "raised and locked" position.

It was a narrow drive with barely enough room for ordinary vehicles to meet and pass. With the stately trees standing on either side and partially overhanging, the sensation was that of traversing a long, narrow tunnel.

A small dashboard signal lamp lit up and began flashing green, signaling "Fire Enable."

He rocked the floor control several degrees left, then corrected the elevation and held the target centered in the range marks as he cruised slowly along the "tunnel."

Target One was the gate itself, a heavy iron affair

170

with massive sideposts—center-opening, chain-locked, manned by a squad of heavily armed sentries.

The two "delegation" vehicles were pulled neatly right and as far forward as they could get, doors open.

Two guys stood between the vehicles, parleying. The others were inside, apparently preparing to take off. Exhaust smoke from the idling engines was finding limited dispersal into the damp atmosphere of the evening, drifting like thin fog just above the cars.

A buzzer sounded from Bolan's console, signifying the approach of maximum depression for the roof-mounted rocketry.

Some guy was running toward the gate from inside the walls, and the two boys parleying between the vehicles were now sending their attention Bolan's way.

The iron gate was dead-centered in the viewplate, Bolan's ankle stiff and holding it there. At a hundred feet out, he banged his knee with a fist to send the first whizzer streaking on ahead, a rustling tail of flame pushing it straight down the tunnel and whomping into the gate with a thunderous roll of fire.

Both limousines were immediately engulfed in that hell, disappearing behind flame and smoke.

Bolan's other foot pushed the accelerator to the floorboard; the battleship on wheels leapt forward in eager response, rushing headlong to join that game down there.

And, yeah—it was a bloody, bloody Monday.

22: KNOCKOUT!

He banged in under the cover of hellfire and brimstone, sending the warwagon plunging through the shattered gates and pressing on without letup along the drive and toward the house.

Wild men brandishing guns and shouting from distorted faces rose up in his path and fell tumbling along the backtrack, beneath the wheels, or bouncing off into the darkness, crushed and broken.

Gunfire rattled across the night and from every quarter, angrily sizzling slugs punching into the skin of the charging vehicle or singing hornetlike across its path.

Target Two found its rightful place behind the range marks, dispatching Rocket Two with another shattering, matter-disintegrating explosive storm to rage into the front entrance of the old mansion, tumbling men and weapons and all that stood there into a shattering chaos of screaming and shouting and thundering hell on earth. Anxious flames leapt immediately skyward to eat the visible heart of an empire and to send ghastly shadows dancing like devils on the future gravesite of its emperor—while, to the west, the enemy engaged itself in the last desperate stand for New Orleans. Machine-gun fire chattered across those doomed, damned acres down there—punctuated now and then with shouted commands and an occasional boom of heavier munitions.

The dreadnought on wheels careened on around the circular drive, avoiding the fiery wreckage of the portico to bounce out across the carefully tended lawn, then to wheel about for a lock-on to Target Three—an upper story window at the south corner east. Bolan banged his knee from three hundred feet out, then was out the door and trucking on over to their place by the time the firetailed serpent struck again, this time to dislodge a corner of their place and send it raining earthward, disgorging shrieking men and dismantled bodies in company with shattered furniture and flaming fabrics.

A secondary explosion of uncertain origin—perhaps escaping natural gas mixing with hell's flames —rumbled through the interior of the old structure and sent more fire and smoke puffing from shattered windows.

Bolan found the upper half of Rocco Lanza face up in a flower bed at the southeast corner. Several feet away lay the broken body of Richard Zeno beside an unidentifiable lump that had probably once been a dumpy little man who carried around well-chewed but unlit cigars, one of which was still clamped in a death grip between the teeth.

Other bits and pieces of once-living flesh littered

the area—but there was no sign of the old man who'd wanted only to be buried here.

Bolan went in through the gaping flame-wreathed hole that had once framed a brass-plated door, and he found Marco Vannaducci halfway to the top of a polished mahogany stairway, hairless head bloodied and blackened but still alive and aware, clinging to the railing and struggling to hoist himself upright.

"I ain't goin' nowhere," the old man muttered.

"That's right, Marco," Bolan said. "You're not."

He pumped him cleanly between flaring eyes with the thundering .44; the real king of Mardi Gras and everything else in New Orleans died as he had lived —struggling to survive.

Frank Ebo appeared at the head of the stairs, swaying, blind and bleeding and crying out in a dying voice, "Marco! Marco!"

"He's here, Ebo," the Executioner said, and he gave the faithful shadow what he'd given the old man. The impact of the hit sent shards of skull exploding and pitched him backwards into the flames.

Bolan grabbed Vannaducci by the foot and pulled him clear of the fast-developing inferno, depositing him on the lawn with a bull's-eye cross on the chest, then went on seeking other game.

He found it immediately, less than twenty yards down-country, in the rag-a-tag remnants of a once-proud hardforce, six of them, battered and bloodied and disarmed and dragging themselves back toward the ruins of empire.

They came to a flat-footed halt at the sight of the impressive figure in executioner black. One of the guys declared, in a dismal voice. "Oh, shit, it's you, Bolan."

"It's me," the ice man confirmed. "How's the battle?"

"Terrible. Cops jumped in down there—shit, I guess all the cops in Louisiana."

"You're Johnny Powder?"

"Yeah. Let us go, guy. We've had it."

"So go," Bolan commanded.

He wheeled around and returned to the warwagon, fired her up, and wheeled on out along the reverse track, picking his way through the litter of warfare, past the shattered gate and flaming automobiles, up the tunnel and picking up speed fast.

One punch-out rocket remained, his withdrawal edge—but not needed, now. The caravan from Mississippi was on the move and running west along River Road—probably by some prearrangement of battle tactics. Which bothered Mack Bolan not a whit; he knew what they would encounter down there.

He hit the road and powered east, fired up the monitors for the police frequencies, and began his soft withdrawal toward the relative sanity of New Orleans in Carnival.

Thank God it was done.

EPILOG

He was running east and apparently free on Airline Highway when he switched off the radio monitors, lit a cigarette, and began breathing like a human being again.

The beeping of the mobile phone stole into the moment to startle him. It had never beeped before. It should not be doing so now—a guy in Bolan's situation did not go around handing out his telephone number—not even a mobile one.

He ignored it for a full minute—then sighed and took the call.

A delightfully familiar voice did not give him time to announce station but surged right through on the pickup: "Are you all right?"

"Yes, I'm okay," he told Pol's kid sister. "How'd you get this number?"

"I was in there once, wasn't I?" she replied lightly. "Think I'd leave a thing like that undetected?"

Bolan chuckled tiredly and told her, "I'm headed out, Toni."

"Out where?"

"Maybe west, maybe east. Wherever the sun is red, I guess."

"Without even a rest?"

"I rest as I run," he said simply. "The guys are okay, eh?"

"Oh, sure. They're already experimenting with bland soups."

"Great. Uh . . . we already said our goodbyes. So . . ."

"Think I could sell something to a tired soldier?"

"Like what?"

"Like an interesting, cultured, and scintillating chauffer? For free? Just food and sack?"

He sighed. "No way, Toni, sorry."

"For part of the way? A hundred miles? Ten?"

Bolan laughed softly. "I'm not exactly safe traveling company. People shoot at me and stuff like that."

"How awful. Why don't you change your way of living?"

"Can't. Not without also changing my way of dying. I'm sticking with proven success."

"I see what you mean. Okay, could I sell you one block? One damn block. You can pick me up, same place, I'm here now."

He sighed and told her, "One block stretches to two, Toni, then to three and four. First thing you know . . ."

"Listen, guy! You haul your ass over here and pick me up, dammit!"

He laughed again and said, "Aw, Toni . . ."

"I mean it! I'll blow the whistle on you, guy! I'll

call that ferocious Lieutenant Petro and give him your damn secret phone number!"

Bolan laughed for his own benefit, sighed, and relented. "Okay. Sold. I'll be there. Same corner. Twenty minutes, if Carnival hasn't completely engulfed the area by now. You ready to travel?"

"Got my shoes, my purse, my pants, and my nightgown. Will I need anything else?"

"Just a brave heart, Toni."

"Well you've got enough of that for both of us. I'll be here. You'd better be here, too. Please. Hurry."

She hung up, leaving Bloody Monday and all that it signified to resettle into the conqueror's mind and churn around in there.

Hell, face it, every day was Bloody Monday.

And every town had its equivalent of *empire* lurking somewhere just out of sight and awaiting its chance to spring forth from its own bloody ground.

Brave heart?

"Soft mind, Toni," he muttered to the emptiness surrounding him.

But not tonight. Not for the rest of this night, hell, no.

He took a reading from his watch and translated it to his location on the sector display.

Sure, he could make the corner of Claiborne and Canal in twenty minutes.

Hell . . . he'd make it in ten.

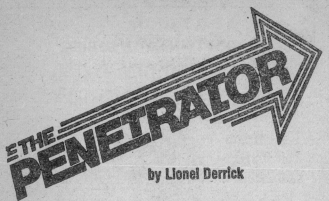

THE PENETRATOR

by Lionel Derrick

Mark Hardin. Discharged from the army, after service in Vietnam. His military career was over. But *his* war was just beginning. His reason for living and reason for dying become the same—to stamp out crime and corruption wherever he finds it. He is deadly; he is unpredictable; and he is dedicated. He is The Penetrator!

Read all of him in:

TO ORDER

Violence is a man!
His name is
Edge...

The bloodiest action-series ever published, with a hero who is the meanest, most vicious killer the West has ever seen.

It's sharp —
It's hard —
It's EDGE

GEORGE G. GILMAN

THE "BUTCHER,"
the only man to leave
the Mafia—and live!
A man forever on the run,
unable to trust anyone,
condemned to a life
of constant violence!

Order		Title	Book #	Price
_____	# 1	KILL QUICK OR DIE	P601	$1.25
_____	# 2	COME WATCH HIM DIE	P602	$1.25
_____	# 3	KEEPERS OF DEATH	P603	$1.25
_____	# 4	BLOOD DEBT	P604	$1.25
_____	# 5	DEADLY DEAL	P605	$1.25
_____	# 6	KILL TIME	P606	$1.25
_____	# 7	DEATH RACE	P607	$1.25
_____	# 8	FIRE BOMB	P608	$1.25
_____	# 9	SEALED WITH BLOOD	P609	$1.25
_____	#10	THE DEADLY DOCTOR	P610	$1.25
_____	#11	VALLEY OF DEATH	P611	$1.25

AND MORE TO COME . . .

TO ORDER

Please check the space next to the book/s you want, send this order form together with your check or money order, include the price of the book/s and 25¢ for handling and mailing to:

PINNACLE BOOKS, INC. / P.O. Box 4347
Grand Central Station / New York, N.Y. 10017

☐ CHECK HERE IF YOU WANT A FREE CATALOG

I have enclosed $_____ check_____ or money order_____
as payment in full. No C.O.D.'s

Name_____

Address_____

City_____ State_____ Zip_____
(Please allow time for delivery)